Endorsements

"*The Soul Catcher* is a mosaic novel packed with resilience and grief, magic and violence, love and loss. Bhide brings India to the page, wrapped in a beautiful sari but with tears in its eyes, a prayer in its mouth, and blood on its hands. This is a narrative about blessings that are curses and how pain changes us. A must read."

—Gabino Iglesias, author of *Coyote Songs*

"I couldn't stop reading this haunting, beautifully written book. Like a fairy tale, it begins with death and ends with life; Bhide's wise and empathetic voice guides us along the way, taking us on a journey through a series of interconnected lives, weaving them into an unforgettable story of love, redemption, and above all, kindness in all its forms—even the one we fear the most."

—Annia Ciezadlo, author, *Day of Honey: A Memoir of Food, Love, and War*

"*The Soul Catcher* will grab your attention and seep into the corners of your imagination from the very first page. Monica Bhide has woven a tale that sharply explores of the emotions we all face as humans moving through a sometimes confusing world. Rife with rich imagery of an India that is at once real and fantastical, this magical novel will draw you in, hungering for more until every last page is turned."

—Ramin Ganeshram, author, *The General's Cook: A Novel*

"Expect the unexpected in this rich novel from Monica Bhide. Shimmering prose is a hallmark of Bhide's writing and nowhere is it more true than this novel."

—Mollie Cox Bryan, Agatha and Daphne du Maurier Award–nominated author

"Woven together with a tenuous strand of destiny, death, and beyond, *The Soul Catcher*, is a collection of interconnected tales as dark as they are full of hope and redemption. Monica Bhide creates a compelling work that takes the reader through an epic journey through myth and magic that examines our relationship with fear, death, life and love. A must read!"

—Kiran Manral, author

The Soul Catcher

A novel in stories

Monica Bhide

Cover image by Simi Jois, Copyright © 2021
Formatting by Polgarus Studio

Bodes Well Publishing
Please contact publisher@bodeswellpublishing.com about special discounts for bulk purchases

Disclaimer
This is a work of fiction. Names, characters, businesses, places, events and incidents are either the products of the author's imagination or used in a fictitious manner. Any resemblance to actual persons, living or dead, or actual events is purely coincidental.

"If I hold you in my heart, you'll wither;
Become a thorn if I hold you in my eyes.
No, I'll make a place for you within my soul instead
So you'll be my love in lives beyond this life"

Rumi

This book is dedicated to lovers

Thank you for being part of this lifetime and all the others to come.

Your pagali

Dear Natalie,

Enjoy!

2021

Prologue: The Soul Catcher

Yamini's story

The amber flame is tiny and potent. The candle burns slowly, radiating sweet scents of musk and frangipani. The wafting smells give life. But more importantly, and without remorse, they also take it away.

The flame burns steadily this evening. It knows someone is going to die tonight.

Yamini gracefully places the candle in a small golden candleholder. She sets it down on the coffee table alongside fresh white roses in a crystal vase, a well-worn book about the Vietnam War, and a jar filled with Christmas cookies. She has been here before and knows the room well. It's filled with photos of his life. A few show him and his buddies on their ship, there are two photos with his sons, and one with his wife, Janet, taken on their wedding day sixty years ago, as she told Yamini.

***

Janet had said to her earlier that week, "It's so nice for a young woman like you to volunteer here. Now tell me: What does your name mean? It is so unusual."

Yamini smiled; it was a question she was often asked. "My

1

mother was living in India when I was born. It was a moonless night and dark outside, so they named me Yamini. It means 'night'." Yamini paused as she saw Janet's reaction.

"What kind of a parent names their child after darkness?" Janet asked.

"She told me that it isn't always the light that brings good things, sometimes the darkness can bring better things in life," Yamini had responded with her ever-playful smile. It was the energy of that smile that had made Janet trust everything Yamini said.

In just a few minutes of conversation, Yamini heard what she needed.

"We decided to bring Tim here because it's time for us to let him go. He's my high school sweetheart, you know? I know in my heart he's ready to leave now. I just need to make him as comfortable as I can." Janet gazed lovingly at her dying husband. It confirmed what Yamini knew already. These souls came to her in dreams. She always knew who was ready to leave and she arrived to assist. It didn't hurt to have the fact verified, not that it mattered anymore. A part of her always died with each soul. But as fate often reminded Yamini, this was her purpose in life. When she was young, she felt powerful. So powerful she could hold her own against defiant cosmic energies, turbulent Goddess manifestations, and even the Universe itself. Then she fell into a doomed love affair. Everything changed after that. Now, Yamini arrived when needed to merely fulfill her duties. The desire to shine and change the world had smoldered away in the seared embers of her broken heart.

***

Now the old man on the bed stirs and calls for his wife. "Janet, is that you? Janet?" The room is dim but for the orange glow of the golden candle.

Yamini moves slowly toward the old man. Her breathing evens out. She centers herself, feeling each breath reach her heart, which opens up and releases some of the pressure she feels to make sure everything is done according to the mandated rituals. One misstep and the man would needlessly suffer.

"I can do this," she mutters, and reminds herself she's done this hundreds of times before. She has to hurry now. There is little time left. She places her handbag by the bedside.

The scents from the candle work their way into every crevice, finding their destination.

Yamini is grateful the bed is low. She sits beside Tim and holds his cold, wrinkled hand. He whispers his wife's name as he struggles to catch his breath. Yamini can feel the love in his aura. Despite his illness, the aura is steady.

"Tim, thank you for calling me. I am Yamini. You appeared in my dream and asked for relief. I am here now, and I promise you will not be in pain anymore," she says, placing a manicured hand on his forehead.

He grips her other hand tightly and opens his eyes. "You have come," he mumbles. "Say goodbye to Janet? I will be hers again. But for now, it's time to go." He barely finishes the sentences, coughing and huffing and puffing between words.

"She feels your love. You have given her remarkable memories. I see them manifested in her cells. They will keep her blissful until you are united again."

She tries to smile at him, but the pain sears through her chest and legs, and Yamini flinches. The irony of it all. The pain she feels can only be relieved by another's death.

When Yamini was five years old, Kalki, a spiritual healer in Shahajahanabad, told her, "When the visions come, you have to act on them. Otherwise you will die a slow, painful death. You will spread light through your darkness. You are the soul catcher." Kalki, with her bald head, large red markings across her forehead and crimson robes, intimidated little Yamini. The same healer had prophesized that Yamini's sister, Damini, would be the healer of pain. It seemed so unfair: One sister kills, the other heals. But such is fate—it doesn't discuss or offer alternatives. Fate decides.

And now here she is, the soul catcher, a hundred years later. Yamini closes her eyes and begins to chant a soft verse of love and living forever, of dying and being reborn, of giving and gratitude. Her mother made her memorize the Sanskrit verses. "The sounds of the words matter, the pacing matters, the pronunciation matters. It is like you have been handed fire. If you don't handle it with care, it will burn you and everything around you."

Young Yamini merely repeated the words without paying attention to the vibrations of the sounds. Then, a child whom she was reciting the chants over died. In a quick second, it was all over. That night, Yamini struggled with falling asleep. When she finally closed her eyes, Kalki in all her glory seemed to appear in a dream.

"I warned you about the powers given to you. You have failed. From this night on, for the next three thousand six hundred and fifty nights, you will not be able to close your eyes in peace. There will be only darkness. I take away your power to imagine."

For ten years' punishment, the soul catcher lost her ability to dream. The nights were unbearable as she'd sit and stare at the ceiling as no thoughts were allowed to enter or leave her mind. After that mistake, Yamini never again took her duty lightly. She practiced the chants day and night, the rhythms of the verses, the vibrations of the syllables, the movements of her hands.

The dreams returned.

Now she begins to chant slowly, savoring each word, ensuring the sound comes from deep within the center of her heart. Slowly, the words flow. Her head sways as the soft hair cascading down Yamini's back appears to move like waves caressing the seashore. The verses reach a crescendo as her mind, soul, and spirit all align. The final verse transforms into karmic energy.

She stops chanting.

From the center of the old man's forehead a cool sensation moves up Yamini's hand and into her heart.

It is time.

She opens her eyes—and Tim closes his forever.

"Thank you for your help," she whispers, and kisses his forehead.

The flame dies. The scent is gone. The only smell that lingers is the lemon cleaning liquid used to mop the floors earlier that morning. Everything is the same, yet everything is different.

Yamini picks up the candle and its holder and places them in a sleek leather pouch.

"Please, come in, we cannot delay," Yamini calls out, and a young man, Andrew, opens the door and rushes in with a wheelchair. The glow from the light in the corridor spills onto the wooden floor.

Andrew grimaces when he sees the silhouette of the man on the bed. It's too dark to see anything clearly.

"Is . . . is that him?"

"Now, now, we need to go, we don't have time," Yamini says, and bends over as the pain worsens.

"Are you okay, Yamini?" Andrew touches her shoulder as he struggles to get Yamini's petite frame into the wheelchair. She looks frail, almost waif-like, yet he can't lift her. He pulls with all his might. He can barely move her. He takes a deep breath and tries again. On the third attempt, he finally gets Yamini off the bed and into the wheelchair.

Yamini can barely open her eyes. She nods gently.

Andrew mutters to himself as he wipes away the droplets of sweat from his forehead, "I need to move. It's okay. This is all going to be okay."

She had warned Andrew that they would have only a few minutes before the hospice staff was alerted about the death. She knew their routine. They would be in at nine to check on Mr. Wilson.

He peeks out the door. The staff is busy watching TV and bantering about Christmas reindeer and how Rudolph is actually a female reindeer since a male reindeer would lose his way.

The hospital where Andrew's young wife is dying is about twenty minutes away. He scans the corridor to make sure no one is looking and then pushes the wheelchair as fast as he can. He's at the end of the hallway when he hears the commotion behind him. He stops and turns around.

"Poor Mr. Wilson. And on Christmas Eve," says a woman dressed in a loud holiday sweater.

She doesn't seem surprised; after all, this is a place where people come to die.

"I think we should wait to call Janet. She just left to be with her grandson twenty minutes ago," says a different female voice. A short discussion decides the action. "I'll go and call her, and you call Fred at the funeral home."

Andrew doesn't want to hear more. He rushes towards the exit. He's heard enough. The man is dead.

"Lord, please forgive me, please forgive me." His muttering gets louder the faster he pushes.

The security guard at the exit catches Andrew by surprise. "Sir? Sir, are you okay? She seems like she's sick. You need help?"

Andrew is startled. He stops, unsure what to do next. Yamini, slumped in the chair, is withering in pain, drooling saliva from the sides of her mouth.

This is no ordinary hospice—this is where the rich come to die. The reception area has shiny floors, a chandelier dripping with crystals, green sofas with white silk cushions, and red poinsettias all around. And they have a full-time guard. With a gun.

The security guard bends down to examine Yamini's face closely. "I know I've seen her here before, same thing each time; she comes in looking fine, and then some dude is always wheeling her out. What's up with that?"

Andrew stares at the guard standing between him and the exit. There is no other way out. On the left is a mammoth, well-decorated Christmas tree with wrapped boxes under it, and on the right is the guard's table.

"Sir, I am asking you again, do you need help? Is she okay?"

"Yes, she's fine. She . . . she's ill, so she sleeps sometimes," Andrew lies as he begins to sweat more profusely.

"Are you sure? Man, she looked fine when ya'll came in. She wasn't in no chair then. Just like before." The guard is now staring at Yamini slumped in the chair. Her striking pink blouse is tight, revealing a perfectly shaped bosom; her jeans are tucked into high-heeled boots.

"Nothing's wrong, I don't know what you're talking about. We have never been here before."

"Listen, man, whatever is going on, you need to tell me before I call the front office." The guard instinctively moves a hand towards his pistol.

Andrew squirms in his jeans and sweater. "I'm telling you. It's nothing. I mean . . . she's my sister and we just visited my uncle. He is ill and she gets very upset when she sees him. She will be fine. That's it, man. We just came to see him for Christmas."

The guard eyes them skeptically. "I *know* I've seen her before. I don't know about you, but I've seen her here before. Sir, I think you better wait here, I'm going to call my supervisor."

Yamini stirs and moves her hand a touch. Suddenly, the guard's attention is diverted. There's a loud noise from the back of the building.

"Sweet Jesus, that sounds like a gunshot! Wait here, I'll be right back." The guard rushes inside.

"Now run," whispers Yamini. "Run, Andrew, *run*. We don't have much time. I can't carry this soul too much longer."

Andrew breaks into a run, pushing as fast as he can, the weight of the chair getting heavier and heavier. The night is dark, with no moon and it seems like no stars.

He struggles to get Yamini in the car, pulling her by the arms and then lifting as he would a small child.

Andrew moves the wheelchair to the side of the parking lot.

They hear the security guard calling, "You! I told you to wait. Hold on there." But Andrew and Yamini are already in the car.

Yamini urges Andrew to hit the accelerator, and the car takes off into the night.

Andrew keeps asking, "Yamini, are you alright? God, what have we done—"

"We will save your wife. Now hurry. I don't have much time. I cannot hold on for too long," she says, and closes her eyes.

In just a few moments, they arrive at the hospital. Visiting hours are over, but the ICU allows family to come in at any time. Andrew places Yamini in a folding wheelchair that he had kept stashed in his car in preparation for this part of the ritual.

"I know it's just supposed to be me, but today, just once, please, just once? It's Christmas Eve and this may be the last time we're together. My sister here is very ill and this may be our last visit with her," Andrew pleads with the night staff to let him and Yamini in to see Mary.

Mary lies on the hospital bed, but it's hard to tell there is a person buried under all those tubes.

Tears roll down his cheeks as Andrew looks at Mary. It feels like each time he comes in to see her, the tubes have multiplied. The air in the room is dead, as if awaiting Mary to join its lifeless state.

***

During one of Andrew's recent hospital visits, he was sitting in the cafeteria, sipping coffee and staring at a piece of paper in his hand. Mary's doctor had given it to him and said, "Her body is shutting down, one organ at a time. I think you should consider signing this."

It said DO NOT RESUSCITATE.

"You can save her, you know, you don't need to sign that paper," said a young woman. Andrew looked up at the stranger seated across the table.

"I'm sorry, do I know you?" Andrew asked.

Yamini smiled. "No, you don't. But I know you. I know your wife is dying and I know how to save her. I can help."

"I'm not interested in whatever it is that you're selling." Andrew stood up to leave. "My wife is dying and you're trying to scam me? Really? This just sucks."

"Andrew, please stop. I'm not trying to sell you anything. If you walk away, you will lose your only chance to save Mary. I know her kidneys have shut down. I know her lungs are filled with water. I know her liver is failing. I know she hasn't opened her eyes or moved or said a word in six days and they don't even know why she is dying. I know it all. I can help."

"How the hell do you know our names—or Mary's condition? I should report you. Who the hell do you think you are?" Andrew stood sternly, hands firmly at his sides. A tall man, he towered over Yamini.

"I can help Mary live a long and healthy life," she said softly.

"What kind of a horrible woman are you? My wife is dying and you're offering me an impossible dream? The doctors have suggested that I take her off life support. It's over. Do you hear me? Over."

"Okay, fine, have it your way. If it's over, then how does it hurt you to give me a chance to help her? I'm not asking for anything in return. Just that you trust me. I can help you."

Andrew stared long and hard at Yamini. Her dark hair was thick and wavy, her eyes sparkled. She could be a model, if it weren't for that fact that she could barely reach over the table. Dressed in a well-tailored suit, Jimmy Cho shoes, and Coach bag, she didn't appear to be in need of money.

"Let me help you, Andrew."

Andrew took a deep breath and sat back down.

"What can you do to help her? I'll give you all that I have if you save her. I have a small house and some cash. I can give you everything. I mean . . . I can't believe I am asking you this. Can you really save her?"

"I don't want your money."

"Then why? I mean, can you really help? Don't mess with me right now."

"I can. Now listen to me. My name is Yamini."

***

And now, here they are, at Mary's door.

The night nurse enters where Andrew is standing with Yamini in the wheelchair. She isn't pleased. "Andrew, Mary isn't doing well. She's in critical condition, you know, and I cannot let anyone who is ill visit her." The nurse looks at the sweat on Yamini's face and shakes her head.

"Please, just this once, we'll never be able to say goodbye. I feel like her time has come," he says and begins to cry.

Yamini opens her eyes. "Please. I love her so. I just want to say goodbye."

The nurse relents. It's Christmas Eve and death seems worse on the holidays.

"I'm so sorry. I wish things were better," the night nurse says gently. She leaves Andrew and Yamini in the room and closes the door.

Yamini manages to get off the wheelchair and begins dragging herself toward the bed.

The whizzing machines and beeping sounds filling the room unsettle Andrew and he finds himself crying again. Mary should be surrounded by the sound of laughter, crying babies, and birds singing, not this.

Yamini turns to Andrew. "Please give me a few minutes alone with her."

Andrew stands there, unsure of what to do.

"Andrew, I cannot hurt her. I won't hurt her. I promise. She's already almost gone. What harm will it to do to give me five minutes alone with her?"

Reluctantly, Andrew goes to leave. He stops and turns back to Yamini. "Please. She is my whole life."

Yamini smiles. She turns back to Mary and waits for the sound of the closing door.

This time the candle flame burns bright. It's strong, steady, and glittering. The sweet scent fills the room and mingles with the smells of bleach and decaying flesh.

Yamini grips Mary's fingers with one hand and places the other on Mary's forehead. The sensation passes from Yamini into Mary's body and her hand begins to feel warm.

Yamini sings her song again, this time with a smile. The chants are slower this time. Rhythmic. Calming. Mary's breathing begins to settle as it synchronizes with Yamini's chanting. Both women begin to breathe in tandem. Inhaling to the mantra of love and life, and exhaling to the words of gratitude. As Yamini watches, Mary's breath become steady; she understands that Mary is ready and willing. This dancing of breaths, entwining and coming together, is the feeling that is most familiar to Yamini ever since childhood. It means one thing for sure: Mary will live, and the excruciating pain will leave Yamini's body.

Yamini's legs feel strong again. She straightens and raises her hands towards the sky. It is time.

With one deep breath, Yamini looks down and blows gently over Mary's forehead. Small, glittering particles, vibrant and life-filled, begin to dance over Mary's face. The merciful energy glows, forming random patterns, and then Yamini recites the final prayer of gratitude. In unison, the particles move down Mary's body and settle into the skin just above her heart.

Yamini has seen this many times and yet watches in wonder.

As the last particle vanishes, Yamini folds her hands in prayer.

"Mercy, my Lord, thank you for your mercy. I am grateful to you, my Lord, I am so grateful."

Yamini blows out the candle and places it in her pouch, and then walks out the door to Andrew.

"By tomorrow morning, she will be fine. Oh—and I have a request."

"What have you done? I *knew* it. I knew you wanted something. Is she okay?"

Andrew tries to look into the room, but Yamini blocks his way.

"Name your first-born daughter Radha. Radha is the epitome of eternal love. Your and Mary's child will bring eternal love into the world. That is my request."

With that, Yamini moves aside and bows to Andrew.

Andrew stares at her. There is a glow on her face and Yamini looks peaceful and, oddly enough, younger than before. She turns and begins to walk away.

Andrew watches her. It looks as though Yamini is gliding, and a few minutes ago she was in a wheelchair, hardly able to move. He shakes his head. Perhaps his tired mind is playing tricks on him. This woman seems certifiably crazy. Here Mary is dying and this woman is talking about babies.

He watches Yamini for another few seconds and then rushes to be with Mary.

"I hope I haven't done something stupid," he whispers. Mary looks exactly the same, the same she's looked for the past six months. Andrew moves close, holds her hand, and sighs deeply. "I really thought she could do something. I don't know what I was thinking. Mary, I love you. What am I going to do without you?"

Suddenly, the machines begin to beep. Louder and louder.

Andrew clutches Mary's hand. "Don't go, *please* don't go. What will I do without you?"

Another loud alarm goes off and the night nurse comes rushing in.

"Oh, no, no, no, no, Mary, don't *leave* me, Mary."

Andrew is weeping and trembling so hard that he fails to notice that Mary has opened her eyes and is looking at him.

Several nurses and an older man, the doctor on duty, arrive

and begin to remove the breathing tube.

"She's choking," someone yells. Then suddenly, they are all quiet.

Andrew, who has been pushed aside and is standing behind the nurses, falls to the floor.

"Mary, no, no, Mary, you *cannot* die. Mary."

The night nurse walks over to Andrew and places a shaking hand on his shoulders.

"Your Christmas wish seems to have been granted. She's breathing on her own—and look at the machines. All her vitals are normal. I—I don't know what's going on. She's breathing on her own."

***

At the other end of town, Yamini returns to the hospice. It is an unscheduled visit. She realized after her visit that the guard was getting a bit too attentive in noticing her previous visits. She decides to check him out, once and for all.

"If he listens to reason, I will let him be. If not, as usual, I cannot have witnesses," she reminds herself.

As expected, the guard is standing outside the main door, smoking.

"Hi there. I was here earlier. Sorry we couldn't wait then."

The guard is clearly startled.

"Look at you, ain't nothing wrong with you. I knew it. Look at you now. I thought you had trouble walking." He stubs out his cigarette. "I need to call my boss."

"Wait, I can explain, just give me a second?" Yamini smiles, her glow brighter now, black eyes glittering.

"You got thirty seconds and don't try anything smart."

"No, I won't. I am a believer in peace and a messenger of God."

The guard nods uncomfortably; she's beginning to weird him out.

"At least can we go inside? It's freezing out here and my clothes aren't warm enough," she says, walking towards the entrance.

He follows, unsure at first, reaching for his pistol to make sure it's there. "I have a gun. Godammit, I have a gun. I am fine. I have a gun," he mumbles.

"Can we sit at your desk there?"

The guard shakes his head. Yamini turns to him. "Come on now. Let me at least try to explain."

"I don't trust you." He is adamant.

"But you have a gun. What can I do?" She's beautiful and coy, and he's taken in.

He nods and sits down at the desk. She sits across from him.

"Make it quick, I don't have all night. What's the deal with the wheelchair, and am I right? You know, the *last* time you left, someone died. I thought nothing of it. It happened again tonight, lady. What the fuck is going on?"

Yamini is studying his face.

"I don't have all night. Answer my damn questions or I'm calling my boss. Something about you ain't right."

"What will it take for you to forget what happened? I can make you a very rich man," Yamini offers.

The guard studies her face. "You disgust me. You want me to simply ignore the fact that people die when you come here?"

Yamini tries again. "I can give you three times what you make a year right now. Pretend this never happened."

The guard fidgets with his cigarettes as he watches Yamini intently. He is starting to look angrier and she realizes he isn't going to budge. Now, he is going to lose his life over her stupid carelessness.

Yamini makes a face. "This place stinks of cigarettes. Mind if I light a candle here and then we can talk?"

"What the hell? You want to light a fucking candle? This chat is over."

"Please, it's just to help clear this air. I hate the smell of cigarettes."

"Fine, light your damn candle and then spill it, lady." With that, he takes out his gun from the holster and places it so that Yamini can see he means business.

Yamini places her golden candle on the desk and lights it.

"Smoking kills, you know," she says, as the flame comes alive.

Just as Yamini is about to get started, a vision flashes in front of her eyes.

"What's wrong? You look like you've seen a ghost." The security guard stands up and backs away from her.

Yamini begins to shake.

The soul catcher has seen her next assignment, and this one is personal. She needs to head back to India, the country she left years ago.

The Train to Nirvana

Sehar's Journey

"Listen to me, I'm counting," young Amya's voice bounces off the old stone walls as she and her parents, Sehar and Rishi, clamber down into a deep, large pit.

Rishi stops for a moment to catch his breath. His lungs struggle for air. He tries to find a grip on the wall and takes a gentle breath. He just needs to hold on for a couple of hours longer. His mind reassures and reminds Rishi of the decision he's made: the decision to die.

"Slowly, Amya, these stairs are old and slippery," Sehar calls to her daughter who is already halfway down. The crooked stairs have thick, green moss growing all around them and on the steps. Sehar puts a hand under her nose to try and avoid the stink that appears to be emanating from whatever is decaying at the bottom of the staircase. The stench is a reminder of her youth at the family farm where dead animals were common, thanks to the resident wolves.

"Fifty-three! Mama, what comes after fifty-three?" Amya stops and looks up at her parents. Just above them she can still see the sky filled with the glorious amber of the setting sun. She clutches a favorite, torn blanket in one hand.

"What in God's name is that?" Sehar screeches as something flutters and brushes past. She runs fingers through her purple-streaked hair for comfort. An old habit from childhood.

More bats come out of the deep crevices of the step-well as the family tries to remain calm and continue down.

"I will tell my teacher tomorrow we saw bats on magical stairs." Amya is even more excited now, but all the same, she clutches the blanket a little closer.

"Ma, what is this place called?" Amya asks loudly.

"It is a baoli. A step-well. Remember the story I told you? In olden times, rains would fill this place with water and people would come in to take a bath," Sehar knows that if she avoids answering, Amya will only keep repeating the question again and again.

"I remember. You told me this has one hundred and three stairs. I'm already on stair fifty-eight." Amya claps and, bats forgotten, descends fearlessly into the dark pit.

Sehar moves faster to reach Amya. Rishi leans on the side of the well to steady himself and then begins to slowly descend.

The baoli has no water today. Years ago, this well swelled not just with water, but the laughter and joy of people who adored it. The waters were friendly and inviting. People would stop in to take a bath, meet with friends, and even marvel at all the crevices and arcs built into the stone walls. But over the years, something changed.

The well waters had turned darker than black ink.

"Amya, baby, slow down. I don't want you to fall. Please child, listen." Sehar holds her daughter's hand tightly. The steps are steeper and it's getting darker.

Sehar wants to ask Rishi "Why would you bring us here?" Yet she remains quiet. The energy surrounding the well is disturbing. Like it wants to sink into your skin and suck out any hope.

When the waters turned dark, years ago, the locals began to stay away. The dark waters attracted the sad, the depressed, the unworthy, the unwanted. People would suddenly disappear and, within a few days, their bodies would be found floating in the muddy, black, baoli waters. Incredibly, the corpses always looked peaceful, an eerie smile etched on their faces. The elders forbade children from going to the step-well for any reason. Once a vibrant pool of life-giving water, the well turned macabre.

Over the years, the waters receded and the baoli became just another stop on "The Most Haunted Places of Shahajahanabad" tours. While tour operators joked about all the other haunted sites in Shahajahanabad, this site always came with a disclaimer: "Don't go down the stairs. We will not come down and look for you."

A year or so ago, much to the horror of the locals, the stench of dead bodies returned to the baoli, prompting much speculation.

"There is a smell, but at least there are no bodies," one of the locals complained to the police. After a few dozen calls came in, the police investigated but found nothing.

"The old walls are telling tales, but we don't know how to listen yet," one of the senior officers remarked during a press conference, then announced they were padlocking the main entrance so no one would wander in by mistake and be hurt.

Rishi, of course, had been informed of that, and was instructed to use a hidden entrance on the opposite side of the baoli. The entrance was behind an old palm reader's shop. As they had walked by the store, the sign had made Rishi stop: DEFEAT KARMA. DESIGN YOUR DESTINY. It brought back memories of his first love.

Now he shook it off. That was a long time ago. No time for those memories. Some events are best forgotten.

"One hundred and three. We are here. Mama, I counted one hundred and three steps." The three of them now stand at the bottom of the well. The only light is from the fading sun above.

"Rishi, I smell jasmine—" Sehar whispers. "How is it that this place smells like death at the top of the stairs and life at the bottom?"

"I'm scared, Mama, I don't want to be here." Amya suddenly clutches her mother's leg as she notices dark stains on the ground.

Rishi carefully moves forward towards the wall. He uses the light from his phone to see if he can locate an electronic keypad he's been told is there.

He struggles to find it as he randomly pushes on the small stones.

"This was a bad idea. I told you. We need to leave now, Rishi. Stop this madness now," Sehar says, looking at the stairs. Rishi could barely make the journey down, and Sehar worries how he will make it back up.

"Please. Just give me a moment. There is supposed to be a keypad here," he says, and moves the flashlight slowly as he searches for the elusive keypad.

"There—there it is, look at the bottom. Papa, I see it, there it is," Amya squeals with excitement, the fear of the darkness forgotten again as quickly as it appeared.

"Can I please punch in the numbers? I want to, can I? Please, Papa, can I?" Amya is stubborn and insistent. Rishi relents.

"Okay, but you have to do it slowly. Punch in the number I tell you and then stop. Okay?"

She nods. 2-3-8-5-3-2.

The numbers are punched in. Rishi checks to make sure the code is correct. He then tells her to push the "enter" button.

Nothing happens.

Rishi hits the button again. Nothing.

"Papa, maybe you should say, 'Open Sesame?'" Amya whispers, recalling her favorite tale, "Ali Baba and the Forty Thieves."

"Rishi, we need to leave now. This is a sign from the Universe. Come on, please, stop this madness," Sehar says, placing one hand on her thumping chest.

"Mama, look." Amya points and both Rishi and Sehar turn. The dark, old wall behind them slides open and they find themselves staring at a large white room.

"Mama, come on. Let's go." Amya pulls her mother's hand and they walk in. The wall closes behind them.

"Where is Ali Baba?" Amya asks. Sehar just shakes her head and takes in the strange, chilling sight.

The rectangular room is empty except for two abstract red paintings on the stern white walls. No signs, no phones, no people, nothing else.

Rishi looks around, unsure what to do next. Amya is still asking for Ali Baba. Sehar hold back her fears—the bright room is sterile and the energy is even more terrifying than the dark baoli steps.

Rishi notices that there is a button on one of the paintings. He pushes it gently. Behind them, the wall lifts and there is a full-size sliding glass door. The area beyond is filled with chic white couches dotted with ritzy golden pillows. Vases with white lilies sit atop low side tables. Sleek sconces on the walls hold glittering candles. The flowers and the lights give the room the feel of a luxury spa.

There is an oddity, one that sends chills down Sehar's spine. It's the oddity Rishi thinks he needs, the oddity that makes this place an urban legend to those who hear about it. Sehar had been one of the doubters. When Rishi first claimed that a high-end facility had been built under the broken-down, deserted, haunted baoli, Sehar was sure Rishi's medications had started affecting his brain.

But here it is. In real life.

The oddity: the room has only three walls. The front wall has the sliding glass door, the two side walls bear candles, but instead of a fourth wall, there is a huge translucent screen. Beyond the screen is darkness. Rishi moves towards the sliding door to see if he can get a better view. The door doesn't open.

"I can't believe this really exists," he says softly. A piercing pain on his right side reminds Rishi to be grateful for what he's seeing.

Sehar moves towards the glass door, recalling what Rishi had told her earlier: "When the time comes, I will board the train to Nirvana. The journey will take thirty seconds."

"Rishi, we need to leave. This is not for us," Sehar whispers as she tries to hold Amya back. The child, curious, is poking around and looking for the magical button that will surely open the sliding doors.

Unsure of what to do next, Rishi looks around to see if there is someone who can help them.

"Rishi, are you listening to me? We need to leave. I cannot believe this even exists," Sehar says. And yet, here they are, under a thousand-year-old step-well, feeling as though they've stepped onto the set of a high-tech movie.

Suddenly, the sliding door opens. Rishi and Sehar walk in after Amya, who begins to jump on one of the white couches as her parents stare at the translucent screen.

A loud voice announces, "Welcome to the Nirvana Train. My name is Ravi. We spoke on the phone today. You must be Rishi? Dr. Patel is on his way and will be here soon."

The family turns around to see a handsome young man who has appeared from nowhere.

"What is your name, young lady? How old are you?" Ravi kindly asks Amya.

Amya holds up four fingers and grins.

"You must be Sehar?" Ravi says to Sehar. With swollen and puffy eyes, she nods.

"How are you holding up, Rishi?" Ravi asks, looking carefully at who will be getting on the train. Rishi's sunken eyes, hairless head, and starved frame point to one thing: a body ravaged with terminal cancer.

"Well, I was just wondering . . . what happens now?" Rishi asks, pointing towards the translucent screen.

"Ah, yes. Your carriage will arrive in a few minutes. You are all welcome to go in and look around. Then, when the time comes, everyone else will leave—"

Amya says, "I'm going with Papa on the train. I'm going with him, Mama. I *am* going with Papa. Look, I even brought my toothbrush." She produces a pink toothbrush from a dress pocket.

Ravi cringes. He looks at the parents and leans forward to whisper, "We don't encourage children here, but of course, it is your choice."

Sehar begins to weep again. "You can't do this to us, Rishi, you can't leave us here and go. You are my husband, my life, what am I going to do without you?"

Rishi hugs his wife of five years. Five years of gentle companionship. Who knew just five years would define their time together?

Even as he hugs her, Rishi recalls his first love. Yamini. His exquisite Yamini.

***

"You guys put Romeo and Juliet to shame," friends had declared. Rishi constantly painted beautiful portraits of her. She loved posting selfies with him in the silliest of situations: dunking in a public fountain, trying to catch soap bubbles, throwing glitter on their faces, having her paint his toenails baby pink, or showcasing his nonexistent cooking skills. They didn't care what the world thought, or if there was even a reason to care.

"You both know there's a whole world outside your little romance, right?" was the constant reminder from family and friends. Rishi meticulously planned the wedding proposal. Deep within the bosom of a palatial resort in the city of Jaipur was a particular terrace that Yamini had admired on Instagram. Rishi found the place, called them, and within weeks the two were there. Everything was timed just right: First, the beauty salon took extra time to ensure Yamini looked her best, dressed in a shimmering Rohit Bal gown, her long hair in wavy curls covering the dress's backless top. The parlor staff insisted on taking photos with Yamini, as if they couldn't believe that someone could actually look this beautiful. They told Yamini she was part of a highly confidential magazine shoot for Bal's latest collection—a lie she easily swallowed, because recently Yamini had been getting requests to model for various designers. Despite being tiny, her radiance was so strong that designers had begun begging Yamini to wear their collections on the runway.

Once she was ready, Yamini was told to head to the main terrace for the shoot. She walked onto the marbled terrace under a glittering full moon night. The path was strewn with red rose petals. Oil lamps gave off a warm, romantic glow. When she reached the center of the terrace, Yamini stopped and looked at the larger-than-life, brocade-covered swing set. She sat down, looking around in awe.

Rishi appeared along with her favorite romantic music being piped. He got down on one knee. "There is only you, there will always be only you. And I have this feeling that there was only you. We aren't lovers just from this lifetime. This feels eternal to me."

She said yes. But the happiness was short lived.

One night, quite by accident, Rishi followed Yamini to someone's house. She had forgotten her phone and Rishi wanted to make sure she had it. Something about the way Yamini was behaving made Rishi just follow her quietly, rather than catch up. He saw it all, the candles, the sensual chanting, the orgasmic look on Yamini's face at the death of the person in front of her.

Rishi ran home and was sick several times.

The next day, Rishi told Yamini what he had seen. He didn't want an explanation. He didn't care. He just wanted her to stop. He wanted to marry a normal woman. Not someone who seemed to be involved in some sort of witchcraft. Yamini tried to tell him that it wasn't a voluntary thing. It was her fate. She was the soul catcher.

"Do you know what this means? Do you even understand?" he was saying, waving his hands in the air, terrified. "I mean, what do you *think* you're doing? How can you kill people? Who the hell are you to do this?"

"I—I am—" she tried to speak, but he wouldn't let her get a word in.

Then, when Rishi calmed down after finally hearing Yamini out, he said, "Do you know what happens when two people make love? They exchange physical and spiritual parts of each other. I believe that lovers imbibe each other's karma."

She had nodded.

"Do you know what this means for the souls you are taking on? You are taking on their karmic journey—all the good, the bad, and the terribly dark."

Yamini wanted to explain how it worked, but Rishi had made up his mind.

He threatened that he would tell the media and make it so people stayed away from her. "You are playing with people's souls. Karma is passed along with those souls. You are not a goddess. Don't play one," he told her repeatedly. Yamini wanted to listen, she wanted to give it up, she wanted to marry him. This wasn't a bad habit she needed to break. It was a God-given gift.

But not everyone gets what they desire. Yamini had her own karmic destiny. And so, she kept saving souls, and Rishi made good on his threat and called the media. But he didn't realize what he would unleash. The tabloid press was more than happy to oblige what seemed just another bizarre story of the supernatural. All they heard was she was killing people and stealing their souls. Not a single media person stopped to ask what that meant or how it was even possible. They just took the sensational story and ran with it. Ratings, after all, were everything. A beautiful woman working for the devil? Yes, *that* would satisfy their audience for months. They hounded Yamini, chastised her, made slogans for and against her. They made it impossible for her to even breathe in peace.

The detractors began to appear. The angry and the outraged. Then one night, around three in the morning, Yamini woke up startled. The loud noises outside had stopped—perhaps the protesters had gone home—but something made the hair on the back of her neck stand up. Someone had thrown a stone through the open window with a note.

"We will kill you before you kill again."

Yamini's hands began to shake as she took a picture and texted it to Rishi, saying she loved him and wasn't doing anything wrong.

Rishi replied, "We can love each other, but we can never be lovers again. I cannot take on someone else's karmic burden."

With that Rishi ended the conversation—and their life together.

Rishi was hit hard by what he perceived as a betrayal. He had been raised on Vedic rituals, chanted mantras and prayers, and understood every word of the *Bhagvad Gita*. He believed in the karmic destiny of souls, in the philosophy that human bodies carried memories of ancestors long gone. He thought what Yamini did was vile.

She had argued, "Think of it like a heart or a kidney transplant. Don't those have living energy and karmic ties? Yet you think the doctors who perform those surgeries are healers and Gods. So how am I wrong? I'm saving lives and I only take the souls of those who call me in."

But Rishi would have nothing of it, or anything to do with Yamini. She was a murderer, a killer. The love of his life took people's lives.

After that, Yamini disappeared. She went to the only place that gave her solace, her cousin Divya's home and sanctuary. Yamini often stayed there when life plagued her. Rishi never heard from Yamini again.

The anger settled. Yamini was gone. Rishi's life was vacant, his heart broken. He stopped talking, rarely bathed or ate, and began to waste away. The only emotion anyone ever saw was when he was shown a picture of Yamini. A single tear would roll down his cheek.

Rishi's family intervened quickly and arranged a marriage to Sehar. The union was hard on both of them, as Sehar knew of his love for Yamini. But she loved Rishi and was gentle with him. She started making his tea just the way he liked it, with slivers of ginger. She would read his beloved *Bhagvad Gita* to him at night as he struggled to sleep. When Rishi awoke, his favorite breakfast, along with freshly squeezed juice, would be waiting for him at the table.

"Don't punish me for something she did. I love you. We can make a life together," Sehar told him one morning. Rishi felt ashamed and selfish, and promised to give Sehar all his love. Soon Amya came along and the bond became strong. Amya was filled with pure joy, constantly laughing, curious about life and all its glories, and totally in awe of her father. The feeling was mutual, and Rishi found redemption in his child.

***

"Sir, sir?" Ravi fidgets as he watches Rishi trying desperately to calm Sehar. "I'm so sorry that you have to deal with this. If I can do anything to help, I am here. This is actually my first day here on my own." He instantly regrets saying this when he sees the look on Sehar's and Rishi's faces.

"I mean, I've been here for a year, but today is my first day alone with a client in a room. Please, don't worry. We have taken utmost care for your comfort and . . . and your journey."

Ravi smiles as he had been taught: just enough to show that he understands how difficult the situation is, but not enough to make light of it. Yes, it is the perfectly practiced smile. As much of a smile one can manage announcing someone's impending death.

"Papa, I am going on the train with you. This will be fun." Amya giggles.

"Welcome," a voice booms from the entrance. Everyone turns to see a tall, well-dressed older gentleman.

"Sir! Folks, this is Dr. Patel," Ravi addresses him, and smiles his well-rehearsed smile.

Patel walks towards Rishi, who manages to leave Sehar's side for a moment. Patel hugs Rishi. He then offers his hand to Sehar. She refuses and stares angrily at this messiah of death.

Patel signals Ravi, who gets the hint. He takes Amya by the hand and leads her outside with promises of getting her the biggest ice cream cone ever.

"I'm sorry to meet you in person under such difficult circumstances. Please know that we are here for you and your family. Sehar, we will harvest the organs. We have discovered innovative ways to clean organs after chemo, to sell them . . . that money will help you and Amya. Please, please sit," he motions to Rishi, who meekly sits down next to Sehar.

"I don't want him to do this, Dr. Patel. Do you realize what you're saying? I should try to build a life for my child and me on my husband's dead body? I'm only here because he was going to come without me and I couldn't let that happen. I want you to stop this madness. Please. Stop it now." Sehar sits up straight. Her tone is firm, fierce.

"Sehar, believe me. I understand your pain. This train was never meant for this purpose. I created it for death-row prisoners. But then, my only child, my son . . . he was just ten. There was no other way." Patel stops speaking. He removes his glasses to clean them and then puts them on again.

Sehar grips Rishi's hand.

"My son, my child, was in the final stages of a horrendous, painful lung cancer. No doctor could help anymore. We had reached the limits of human medicine. He'd scream endlessly into the night. God didn't listen, so I did. Now I try to help other people who have no options left. Trust me, Rishi will not feel a thing. He will sit on his seat and within thirty seconds he will go to sleep. What do you wish for your husband? Another few weeks of torturing pain, or a quiet, painless death?"

Sehar stands up, indignant, fuming. Her eyes flash with anger. "You have no right to play God."

"Please, Sehar." Rishi's weak plea doesn't stop her.

"He is my husband. He is the father of my child and you want to kill him. I will never let that happen. What will we do without him?" Sehar is almost screaming.

"Sehar, I am a father and a husband. I sympathize. But this isn't about you or your child. This is about Rishi. Look at him. He has been off his morphine drip for less than an hour, right? In another ten minutes, he will start crying in pain. This is about saving him from that pain. Do you understand?"

Sehar sits down, places her face in the palms of her hands, and weeps. The mention of Rishi's pain always breaks her. When his pain arrives, his body contorts, his orifices leak, his hands tremble, and he begs for mercy. The pain medicine soothes the piercing suffering, but takes away all his senses. He hallucinates, sees blood dripping from the walls, and thinks his hands are scissors trying to cut open his eyeballs.

The medicines meant to help him destroy who Rishi is.

"You tell me, Sehar. Is there another way?" Patel asks.

"Please, Sehar. Don't make this harder than it is. I don't want to leave you and Amya. I don't. But what choice do I have? Tell me. I cannot live like this anymore. There is no cure, no miracle, nothing. Do you understand? This way my death will not be in vain. The money will help. Be practical." Rishi whimpers as the pain begins to return to his legs and stomach.

Patel folds his hands and bows. "I must take my leave of you now. Rishi, Godspeed to you. Sehar, I will be waiting outside." Then he quietly turns around and leaves the couple alone.

"Mama, I got ice cream." Amya bounces back into the room with the remnants of a rather large ice cream cone.

Before her parents can respond, Amya shrieks with pleasure, throwing down her ice cream. "Look, look, the train is here."

The translucent screen slides to the right, revealing a carriage made of glass. There is a single white seat inside and a prayer altar facing it.

"It's time," Ravi says.

Sehar looks at Rishi, silently pleading with him again.

The door to the train carriage opens.

Ravi says, "You will have about a minute, and then the train leaves. You must decide now, as we have no way to stop the train once it starts. I repeat, there is no way to stop this thing. This is it." He bows and then leaves to give them their last minute together.

Amya is already exploring the carriage when Rishi steps inside and Sehar follows.

Sehar pleads, "Please, Rishi, don't do this. Please. I don't care that you have a few days, even a few minutes. Please. Don't tear us apart. I cannot live without you. Please, I am begging you. There are new cures every day. Even your oncologist said there is a new trial that you can be a part of. There is hope."

Rishi, so sure a moment ago, now looks hesitant. He stares at his beautiful daughter, his amazing wife.

The face of Amya laughing dances in front of him, and Sehar with her pleading eyes.

Can I really not bear it just another few weeks? Death was coming for me anyway . . . why not just wait? Am I really that selfish?

"But I will be gone in a few weeks anyway," he murmurs.

"Please, Rishi. I will find a way. It will work out. Please, if you have ever loved me, please don't do this. I'm begging you. Don't do this. You know Yamini can help us. *You know that.* We can call her, please," Sehar moves closer and hugs him.

"I . . . I don't know if I can bear this pain anymore. I can't call her. She will never come after what I did to her. This is my fate. I must die now. I must—" Rishi begins to cry.

"I will be there with you. I will do what I can to make you comfortable. Please, Rishi, please. Don't do this."

A bell chimes and a voice comes over the speaker: Five seconds to the door closing.

"I won't let you do this, Rishi, I *won't* let you do this." Sehar screams in anguish and uses all her strength to pull Rishi out of the train.

They barely make it as the door closes behind them and the Train to Nirvana departs.

"I can't let you go. I'm not ready to lose you. You are my life." Sehar kisses his face through her tears.

Rishi is flooded with a relief of sorts and hugs her back. They cry and hug and kiss.

"Amya, look, Papa didn't go on the train," Sehar says, filled with relief. "Amya?"

Suddenly, a bright blue strobe light flashes and a shrill sound shatters the quiet room. "EMERGENCY. THIS IS AN EMERGENCY."

The carriage returns.

The translucent door opens slowly.

Amya is lying on the floor holding her blanket and toothbrush.

No Cure for Curiosity

Ravi's Journey

"Dr. Patel, we need a firm policy around families in this area. This is a bloody disaster." Ravi's voice shakes as he takes in the gut-wrenching scene in front of him.

"And on your first day alone, no less," Patel says sharply and then ignores Ravi and tries to calm the parents down. The facility has been running smoothly for two years and this is its first major disaster.

Ravi knows this could lead to a shutdown of the facility.

"Why can't parents watch their children?" he mutters, initiating emergency procedures. Within moments, medical personnel, train engineers, and a priest, are all on their way.

Patel is about to call one more person who he thinks can provide some assistance, when Ravi's phone buzzes. Patel is annoyed. "Ravi, please. Do you have no regard for what just happened?"

"I'm so sorry, sir." Ravi excuses himself from the room and much to Dr. Patel's chagrin answers his phone. The caller is his wife, Nisha. Ravi knows the call means she's probably heading into labor to give birth to their first-born. The irony doesn't escape him.

He answers the phone, but his wife has hung up.

He sends her a text: *YOU OKAY? BABY COMING?*

No response.

Ravi hears Patel calling him back to the room and is getting ready to return when his phone buzzes again.

SIR, TT HERE. PLEASE RETURN HOME NOW, reads the text message from Nisha's phone.

TT is the trusted watchman who guards Ravi's house. *What the heck is the watchman of our house doing answering Nisha's phone?* Ravi wonders.

He hears Patel calling again and runs back into the white room. He whispers into Patel's ear that he has his own emergency. Patel just pushes him away, his eyes filled with anger, face livid. Ravi worries that Dr. Patel is upset with him. But such is life, he reminds himself. He wants to say something to Sehar and Rishi before he leaves, but no words come. He simply folds his hands in prayer, bows, and runs out.

TT, WHERE IS NISHA? WHY ARE YOU ANSWERING HER PHONE? Ravi texts back frantically as he runs to the elevator that will take him to the parking lot. He then calls home again. No answer.

Another text message arrives: *RAVI SIR COME NOW.*

Ravi shakes his head. This stupid watchman.

Why can't he just tell me that the baby is coming. This mysterious message is just stupid. I am going to fire him as soon as I get home. Moron.

Ravi tries to call again, his fingers pounding hard on the phone keyboard. He tries to remind himself that Nisha has had a healthy pregnancy so far and that this is just TT being his usual overprotective self. Maybe Nisha was craving some potato chips and the store was out of them. TT did have a tendency to play rescuer and protector, and loved Nisha because he'd been with her since she was a newborn. Ravi stops for a second. Maybe *he* was overreacting and should return to help Rishi and Sehar?

Then another text arrives: *RAVI SIR IT IS BAD*.

Ravi tries to call once again. This time, TT answers.

"Sir, there is trouble. Tej was here."

Ravi shudders and the phone slips and falls from his hands.

Tej, once his friend, is now the local thug.

The phone begins to buzz again. Ravi picks it up off the ground. It's Patel.

"Ravi, where are you? What's going on? You left in the middle of the biggest disaster this facility has ever seen. It is your job to be here," Patel barks into the phone. Ravi can hear others in the background and is relieved that help has arrived.

"It's Nisha. Something's wrong. I n-n-n-n-need to leave—p-p-p-please," Ravi stutters. He had stopped stuttering after he started working with Patel, but it's back now. Nothing like fear to make life real again.

"With the baby? Is everything okay?" Patel softens when he hears the terror in Ravi's voice.

"I'm s-s-s-sorry for what happened here, but I m-m-m-must leave." Without waiting for a response, Ravi hangs up. He reaches the exit and begins sprinting towards his car, his short frame almost flying through the parking lot.

Ravi places his sweaty hands on the steering wheel. It's going to take him an hour to get home, even if he drives as fast as he possibly can. Once the heart of Shahajahanabad, the area where Nirvana Central sits is a ghost town. The center of Shahajahanabad was moved almost five decades ago to an area about thirty kilometers away. Once businesses moved, so did the restaurants, stores, and tourists. All that was left were old buildings, beggars, the odd monument, and the baoli, the step-well that houses Nirvana Central in its belly.

The Nirvana Central security gates are already open and the guard waves wildly as soon as he sees Ravi's white car.

Ravi slows down.

"Go through, no need to stop. All clear," the guard yells and lets Ravi pass.

The car picks up speed, and Ravi's mind is racing faster. He tries to call TT again, but there's no response from him or Nisha. The roads are empty, the sky is pitch-black, and the full moon has not yet risen.

Dark clouds threaten a downpour. Ravi presses on the accelerator.

The phone buzzes with an old Hindu prayer tune. He recognizes the ring tone: Damini is calling. Damini, who Nisha says is the most amazing midwife in the world. Instantly, Ravi's racing pulse slows down a touch. Damini's call indicates that Nisha is in labor. Ravi takes a deep breath. Perhaps his suspicion is right—that TT blew things out of proportion about Tej paying them a visit.

Ravi sighs with relief and answers his phone.

Damini speaks quietly. "Ravi, I am on my way to be with Nisha. Take your time. All will be well." Before he can say one word, she hangs up. *Oh, this woman. Wait, wait, tell me what is going on*, Ravi thinks, but Damini is gone.

***

"Damini is so kind, why aren't you happy about my using a midwife?" Nisha had said early that morning as he was getting dressed for work.

"She's fine, but I don't know why we can't go to the hospital like normal people to have this baby. I mean, what is the point of me making all this money? We can afford to pay for the best hospital in town and yet you wish to go with this woman. She has no medical training. What happens if there's a complication?" Ravi adjusted his white collared shirt and dark-pink tie.

"Trust me? She's good. I get good vibes from her," Nisha said in the sweetest voice.

The memory of the morning with his beautiful wife helped settle Ravi's pulse even more. She had been sitting on the bed in a flowing red nightgown, lustrous dark hair cascading almost down to her ripe belly over very full breasts. He couldn't believe his luck. Nisha was as gentle as she was beautiful. She was deeply spiritual, and there were days Ravi envied her faith.

"What makes you so happy all the time?" he often asked her.

"I don't really know, but I feel like I have this well of love inside my heart that just keeps giving. It's hard to explain." Nisha's responses were always followed by a passionate kiss. In those kisses Ravi could feel her energy. It uplifted him, made his panic transform into peace. Perhaps that was the core of true, eternal love—the ability to transform another into bliss. Now they had a baby coming.

The rest of the conversation that morning had been about Nisha trying to convince him that Damini, the midwife, was the right choice for them. In truth, he didn't need convincing, but he liked to disagree with Nisha. Her earnest ways of making Ravi see her point of view were so endearing. He would've let TT deliver the baby if that's what Nisha felt was the right thing to do.

"You're being silly. I trust her. She has delivered hundreds of babies. We'll be fine." Nisha had smiled and heaved herself off the side of the bed. "I have to tell you though, I will be relieved when this pregnancy is over. My feet are swelling."

Ravi helped Nisha stand and kissed her sweet lips. "I love you and will do what you want. Okay?"

"Yes. Okay. Now off you go . . . are *you* going to be okay today?" Nisha was referring to his gloomy job.

"Yes, I'm okay. Just like I don't understand your Damini, you don't understand Dr. Patel and his vision. So we're even." He laughed despite the serious look that appeared on Nisha's face.

"I don't claim to understand what you do, Ravi. But I know that it serves a bigger purpose and Dr. Patel has been very kind. He's made life good for us. It's just hard for me to understand how you all feel comfortable playing God."

***

Now, in his car, speeding home, Ravi is glad that Damini is on her way to help Nisha with whatever is going on.

The dark road is getting darker, the street lamps barely providing any light. Ravi passes the building that has been touted as the mecca of spiritual enlightenment: a yoga center that brought in illustrious instructors from around the world. Ravi recalls that a year or so ago, he was curious and wanted to check it out given that it was the trendiest place in town. He'd found out accidentally one night. His car tire blew right in front of the building and he'd walked in to ask for some water while he waited for a mechanic. The smell of hash was strong. Everyone walking around looked like they belonged on the cover of *Peace and Love* magazine.

"What exactly are you selling here? This doesn't seem like a yoga center," he had asked the bright young thing at the counter.

"Respite," was the response.

The bright young thing at the counter was Nisha. That was how he met his soul mate.

Ravi tries to call home again. No response.

"We don't play God. We just give people an alternate—" Ravi had said to Nisha that morning, but before he could finish, TT, on duty twenty-four hours outside the house, called via the intercom to their bedroom.

"Sir, Tej and his goons are loitering outside again. Shall I call the police?"

"No, just keep an eye on them. I will be out all day and Nisha is home alone."

Now, as Ravi's thoughts shift to Tej, he begins to feel his body tense and anger rise within his gut.

That fucking Tej. He was trouble. *Why, why, why did I leave her at home alone when I knew he was outside?* Ravi thinks as he replays the conversation in his mind over and over again. His car passes closed stores and restaurants as he gets nearer to home. Despite the air conditioner running at full blast, Ravi is sweating profusely. Using one hand, he takes off his tie and flings it onto the back seat. He opens the buttons on his shirt.

Perhaps he should have called the police that morning.

He and Tej went back a long time. Both of them had been

raised in poor homes, forever struggling for even the most basic of necessities. They used to share cups of tea, stale bread, and bemoan their lives as they watched Bollywood movies showcasing boys having fun with nearly nude girls. Tej always said he wanted money more than he wanted to breathe. His parents were both janitors and the grandest thing that had ever happened in his life was when his father had taken the family out to dinner at an extravagant restaurant, only to be embarrassed by the condescending staff who smirked as the family struggled with the menu written in English.

Ravi's family had been slightly better off. His mother worked as a clerk at a food store and often brought in goodies for their families to share.

The trouble had started when Ravi began working for Patel.

The number one rule of Ravi's employment at Nirvana Central was complete and total secrecy. In fact, Patel had made Ravi sign so many documents that his hand had hurt. Ravi had to finally tell Nisha when she threatened divorce, thinking he was having an affair.

Tej would ask Ravi on a daily basis where the money was coming from, and Ravi would refuse to explain. He told Tej that his own mother didn't know what he did for a living. In truth, his mother made him swear up and down in the temple that he was "not doing anything illegal, immoral, or unethical."

Ravi's mother did demand one specific thing and Ravi had been more than happy to oblige: He bought a small but comfortable flat for Tej who was alone now after both his parents had passed away. Ravi's mother felt great affection towards Tej and often invited him to have meals with her. At his mother's insistence, Ravi had even furnished the flat and set up a bank account for his old friend, promising him that the account would always have enough money so Tej would never need to worry about food or clothing again.

But instead of helping, all the generous actions made their relationship go from bad to worse.

"You give me this cheap flat and you live in a mansion. Why are you hiding things from me? I thought we were friends," Tej asked repeatedly and Ravi simply avoided answering. At first, Tej seemed resigned with Ravi's avoidance but then, one night, things got out of hand.

They had been out drinking and Tej, high on several shots of moonshine, had kicked Ravi quite hard in the stomach, asking him again and again where the "loot" was coming from. Luckily some strangers at the bar rescued Ravi, and he swore never to speak to Tej again. Tej seemed to have gotten the message and stopped calling Ravi.

A few weeks ago, Ravi began to see Tej outside his mansion every now and then. When he was drunk, Tej would bark disparaging remarks if Ravi or Nisha appeared at the gate. Ravi had threatened to call the police, but always hesitated. Today, he regretted that decision.

Ravi slams on the brakes as he approaches a red light. The last thing he needs is to be stopped by the traffic police.

The rain starts, small droplets at first, and then a downpour as the sky rips itself open.

Ravi picks up his phone and tries to call Nisha, TT, and Damini again. No answer.

He checks his watch: it will take another ten minutes to reach home. A lifetime.

Screw the cops.

Five minutes. Now four. He keeps looking at the clock . . . almost there.

His phone sings again, the prayer tune.

"Ravi, please tell your watchman to let me go in. I can help Nisha." It's Damini again.

"Tell that idiot I said to let you go in. What the hell is going on there? Why won't anyone tell me? I am *on my way*. Please do what you can for her." Ravi can hear Damini talking with TT in the background.

"All will be well," she says and hangs up.

He reaches the house just as TT is opening the wooden door to the main house for Damini. Draped in a white kaftan, her hair in a tight ponytail, she looks like an aberration.

He brakes, pulls over, and gets out of the car.

His face is panic-stricken, his half-opened shirt soaked with sweat.

"What the hell happened?" he says to TT as he rushes towards the open door.

"Sir, I just went to the bathroom for a minute, just a minute, and Tej and his goons went inside—"

Without listening to the rest of the story, Ravi rushes to see Nisha.

"What the hell happened? Why didn't you answer my calls? Where is she? Has the baby come?" Ravi is still snapping questions towards TT, who's rushing in behind him.

A bone-chilling scream answers his questions.

Nisha is screeching like an animal being butchered.

Ravi stops in his tracks at the entrance of the room, sweat

pouring down his face, his back, his pants sticking to his legs. As much as he wants to know and wants to help, his fear wins and he simply stands there and then turns to TT.

"Tej threw some chemicals all over her."

How could this happen? His beautiful wife, their baby . . . this was all his fault.

"I am here. Please come in with me." Damini takes Ravi's hand and leads him into the bedroom where Nisha is still screaming. TT follows behind quickly. Damini turns around and shuts the door.

Nisha is lying in her bed, still in her red nightgown, just as Ravi had left her this morning. There is dried blood all over the bed, her stomach looks as though someone had used a peeler and peeled bits of it off. The stench of burning flesh fills the room. She is looking up at the ceiling and screaming unintelligibly.

"She wouldn't let me touch her or take her to the hospital. I tried, but she kept asking for you and Damini, and forbade me from calling the police," TT whispers in a trembling voice.

Damini walks up to the bed. She sits down next to Nisha and takes her hand.

TT slumps onto the floor. "I have failed you, sir. I am so sorry."

Almost instantly, the room feels safer, more subdued. A chill runs down Ravi's back. Nisha stops screaming, closes her eyes, and her breathing is less labored. The room is silent, and suddenly colder.

"I'm here, Nisha. From this moment forward, you will not feel the searing of the acid, you will feel the petals of roses as they massage your belly. You will not feel the burn. You will give me your pain. You will give me your burns. You will give me your screams." Damini holds onto Nisha's hand and begins to chant, repeating again and again, "Your pain is mine."

Ravi wonders what to do. He takes out his phone to call the ambulance, the police, to call somebody—to do *something*.

Then he hears TT say, "Sir, look. This is black magic. "

Ravi looks up from his phone. His brain can't comprehend what he's seeing: the burns on Nisha's belly disappear. He rubs his eyes. Maybe the stress is playing tricks on his mind. A gentle breeze seems to be passing over her body wherever Damini's hands hover. As her hands move, the burns dissolve.

The nightgown still looks burnt, but the smell in the room has changed from charred flesh to fresh roses. The chill is stronger.

Ravi opens his mouth, but nothing comes out. He and TT stare at each other.

Damini moves her hands in a ritualistic rhythm, swaying to the sounds of the beej mantra, the seed sound that works miracles. She breathes softly as her hands move, gently, precisely, healing every single cell in the body of this mother-to-be.

The room gets colder and colder.

Nisha's breathing is now steady, deeper. After what seems like an eternity, but in truth is minutes, the burns are all gone. Damini's hands pat Nisha's head, then her eyes, then her cheeks. She continues until she pats every part of Nisha's body, making sure not a single area is missed. She keeps repeating the word "virohana," to heal. Virohana, virohana, virohana, virohana.

Then she stops to take a breath and signals TT to come to her.

Ravi moves forward too, but Damini stops him.

"No, not yet. We need to finish the ritual. Please, TT, come here."

TT looks questioningly at Ravi. Ravi nods, just as perplexed. His phone rings, the ringtone informs him it is Patel, and he ignores it.

Why is she asking for TT?

"Show me," Damini says in a soft but commanding voice. TT simply stands and stares at her, and shakes his head.

"TT, what is going on? What does she want to see? You better tell me right now." Ravi can feel his blood pressure rising again.

Slowly, TT lifts his shirt and turns to Ravi. There are bruises everywhere. "I tried to tackle Tej as he left, but I couldn't do anything. He kept kicking my stomach. I'm sorry, Ravi sir, you have taken such good care of me and I could do nothing to stop him from hurting your family." TT stares at the floor, lowering his shirt, and wrapping his arms around himself in deep shame. "I could do nothing to help Nisha. She is like my own daughter. I am so ashamed."

"TT baba, please don't say that. I know you did everything you could," Nisha says softly as she folds her hands and thanks him.

Damini holds TT's hand and says, "Please come sit on the bed. Pain is real for all of us, not just those who are rich. I can help you. Subhisaj, heal well."

Ravi just stands there, alternating between gratitude for his wife and baby being safe, to shaking in anger at the bastard Tej. Clearly, Ravi underestimated the jealousy that Tej was harboring.

Damini interrupts his thoughts as she finishes healing TT.

"Ravi, you know there is so much hate in this world. We have to take that hate away. That hate is going to destroy everyone."

The chill in the room begins to disappear. A warm calm settles in.

"Both of them will be fine. Nisha is resting now. I must admit, had we been even a few minutes late, you would have needed my sister and not me," Damini says. Before Ravi can ask what that means, Nisha begins to moan in a loud voice.

"Oh, no. Is her pain back? Is she okay?" Ravi's voice stutters as he begins to shake.

"No, it isn't the acid that is making her moan," Damini smiles for the first time. "The baby is coming. Please get me some warm water and fresh towels as soon as you can."

"But I . . . is she okay?" Ravi says anxiously.

"She will be fine. Now hurry."

Ravi leaves the room. TT comes out behind him and closes the door. Ravi rushes to the kitchen and fills a clean bucket with warm water. TT has already got the towels needed. Ravi goes in and hands everything to Damini.

"I want to be here for the birth as we practiced," she says. "Her wounds from the burn are still fresh, I cannot let you be here and see her pain. I will do my best, but you cannot be in here. Wait outside. I need to make sure the acid did not get to the baby."

For the next hour, Ravi checks his watch every minute. He keeps declining calls from Patel, but then at TT's insistence sends a text to say that Nisha is in labor.

"Ravi sir, the baby will need an employed father," is TT's kind reminder.

49

All Ravi can hear is Damini's humming. He can't make out the words, but the humming is extraordinarily soothing. There is no sound from Nisha and Ravi debates with himself about calling an ambulance as he worries that something is wrong with Nisha or the baby.

Then, as though reading his thoughts, TT's words stop him.

"Sir, this lady in white? She is a magician or a witch, but I have never seen a chemical burn reversed. Tej threw so much of it. It's a miracle her body didn't disintegrate. And my stomach? Look, there is nothing here."

Ravi nods and goes to the sink and splashes cold water on his face. *If this is a nightmare, God, please wake me up.*

He tells TT to go outside and sit at his post, and that he'll call him as soon as there is some news. Just as TT leaves, Ravi hears Damini calling his name.

"Ravi, come in," Damini says as she opens the door. In her arms is a tiny baby, still covered in blood and with a cord hanging.

"Nisha and Ravi, meet your daughter," Damini says.

Nisha's eyes are open and she is smiling.

Ravi rushes up to kiss his daughter and his wife.

"Are you okay? She is beautiful," Ravi's mumbles between tears and smiles and hugs and kisses. "This day could not have been any crazier if I tried."

"Is the baby okay? She isn't hurt, is she?" Nisha asks Damini.

"She's fine. She is strong. She is Shakti."

Nisha sits up on the bed and Ravi is beside her. Damini hands them the baby.

Ravi says, "I don't know how to thank you, Damini. I was

wrong about you. I'm sorry I treated you so poorly. I just don't understand . . . and how—her pain. The burns?"

Damini smiles again.

"We all have a gift we can share with the world. Mine is that I can take other people's pain," Damini says as she brushes her kaftan. Earlier, Ravi had noticed the kaftan had specks of blood from the birth on it, but now it appears clean.

"I can't thank you enough. You have saved my whole world from collapsing, and then given us this amazing blessing. I know Nisha will agree with me when I say we will call this baby Damini, after you." Ravi's words, mixed with joy and exhaustion, are soft and gentle.

"Not, not after me. She is Shakti. She will bring strength to the world. Please give her that name and honor her presence in your life."

Nisha says, "Yes, of course. She is Shakti. Thank you."

"How do we pay you, Damini? You never did tell me that. Nisha, do you know?" Ravi, ever practical, suddenly remembers Damini needs to be paid.

Damini laughs and kisses Nisha and the baby.

"I have done my work here and I must go now. Ravi, to pay me, you will now have to do *your* work. People like Tej. They destroy humanity and our faith in it."

Nisha looks confused.

Ravi knows exactly what he needs to do.

"Before you leave, I must ask you for a favor," he says rather sheepishly. "I know you have already done so much for me, but there is something I know you can do to help." Damini nods and he whispers his desire.

"I will take care of it. Don't worry. All will be well," she says, and then turns her attention back to Nisha.

"Do you want something to eat or drink?" Ravi asks Damini, as Nisha is busy nursing the baby.

"I will take care of her and the baby for now, but I will have to leave soon," Damini says.

Ravi thanks her, makes his way to the living room, and sits down on his purple couch.

First, he calls his mother to inform her of the good news and to tell her to come over immediately to help Nisha. He then calls Patel to share the news of the birth, but there is no answer. Ravi decides not to leave a message about the baby, or his impending plans involving Nirvana Central. He wants to tell Patel directly.

Then he calls the housemaid who had requested the day off. He apologizes for calling her so late in the night, but upon hearing that the baby has arrived earlier than scheduled, the maid agrees to come within the hour to help Nisha and to prepare some hot meals.

Taking a deep breath, he makes the next call. This time, Ravi calls Tej.

"Ya, so finally you are calling me. If you call the police, I will kill her next time," Tej's menacing voice booms on the phone.

"We have learned our lesson. Nisha and I agree that we have to tell you about our secret source of income."

Ravi hears Tej laughing. "I'm glad. After all, we come from the same place. Now, tell me."

"Well, I cannot tell you. I can only show you," Ravi says.

"What? If you are making a fool of me, I swear I will kill her this time and I will kill you, and your mother. I will kill you all and feed your body to my dogs," Tej says, his words slurring.

"No. No, I'm not lying. Listen to me."

Ravi explains as calmly as he can that Tej needs to see the setup in person to believe it, and that it's hard to explain the source of income over the phone. "Come here in the morning at eight. Don't be late."

Damini comes out of the room and says, "Be well." With those words, she's gone.

Ravi hangs up the phone, washes up, and is about to go see Nisha again when the doorbell rings.

His mother pushes through the door and rushes towards Nisha's bedroom. "I can't believe you didn't call me when her pain started! Lucky for you, I had a hunch that today was the day and so I had already left my house much earlier." She stops, turns around, hugs her son, kisses him on the forehead, and rushes to see the baby.

While his mother fusses with Nisha and the baby, Ravi falls asleep on the couch.

***

Exactly at eight o'clock the next morning, Tej arrives. TT, already instructed by Ravi not to stop him, brings him to the front door of the house.

Ravi is dressed and ready, waiting for him at the entrance.

"Welcome. I hope you're ready for your adventure?" Ravi asks as he forces himself to smile.

"I'm ready, but if this is a trick, my *guys* are ready too—and waiting. This better not be a trick, Ravi, or you know me—" Tej glares at Ravi.

"No, it is not. I see you have your suitcase ready. Did you pack everything I told you to?"

"I got my clothes, cigarettes, and some food. Will I need anything else?"

"No, the Nirvana Train is a short ride. You'll love it," Ravi says.

The Pain Killer

Damini's story

The night leaves Damini tired, but she knows what she needs to do now, and the very thought makes her smile. After leaving TT and Nisha pain-free, Damini begins her final journey in this form. She turns to look at Nisha's house one last time.

"Shakti will watch over you," she says and blesses the house. She begins her long walk towards her beloved gardens.

The searing pain that nearly killed Nisha is now inside Damini's body and headed to her heart. If she doesn't reach the gardens in time, that pain will kill her.

As she walks, Damini remembers a conversation she had with Ravi just a few weeks ago. He had been difficult.

"Nisha needs to go to the hospital. Why should we use you?" he asked Damini repeatedly.

"All I know is that when people invite me to help them, there is a deeper reason there. I don't always know what it is and, to be honest, sometimes they don't either. But this world of pain binds me to them. I am here; it's a call of duty," she'd replied. Ravi had reminded Damini of that conversation this evening when he thanked her profusely. He repeatedly apologized for not understanding her role.

Damini quickly pulls out her phone and sends the promised text message.

She looks up at the dark sky. The clouds, their burden spent, are gone. The wet road beneath her bare feet gleams in the dark, glittering under the full honey moon. It comes once every hundred years, this moon, and it's the moon she has been waiting for.

"You are my last pain patient, Nisha," Damini had said to Nisha earlier that night, after the baby was born.

"Last patient? Why? What is wrong?" Nisha said, holding Damini's hand.

"I just want to be a normal person, you know? I don't want this—this thing, this curse, anymore. Tonight is the honey moon. I am to go to the Garden of Harmony and ask Chand, the Moon God, to free me of my bond of pain."

"Why? You're helping so many of us. I don't know what it's like to be you, but if you give up this blessing how will another Nisha ever survive?"

Damini answered with a mere whisper, "My whole life has been for other people. Just this once, I want to live for myself."

They had hugged and Damini said her final goodbye.

"Now, I must hurry. If the sun rises before I reach the gardens, I will have to carry on this path for another hundred years."

Damini hurries more. Her mind shifts to the candid reason she wants to stop being the pain killer: For the first time in her life, she's in love.

The love of her life is a lover of books, a wizard with words, a poet, a painter, and a weaver of wistful fables.

Damini met him a few months ago at the hospital. He needed surgery to remove a malignant tumor from his brain. As they prepped him, they realized he was unresponsive to the anesthetic. The nurse on duty called Sister Angela, and Sister Angela called Damini.

Damini smiled as she recalled that fateful meeting. She took his pain, and he stole her heart. "Your name. I love your name. It defines you. Amrit: immortal," she said, when he thanked her.

"I'm not exactly sure what you did, but I didn't feel a thing during the entire surgery. I just want to know, are *you* okay?" His concern ignited something in her heart. She had helped thousands of people with their pain and while all of them thanked her, not a single person had ever asked how *she* was and how this affected her.

After that conversation, Damini and Amrit were inseparable.

"For the first time in my life, I feel like I am loved for being me instead of my healing powers," she had confided in him. She learned that he was a school teacher and taught English around the world. She was mesmerized by his travels: He had taught under the open skies in Nakuru, on the shores of the impossibly beautiful Padang Bai, in the deep underbelly of Dharavi, on the open terraces of Begur. He was an avid photographer and shared images of the beautiful gardens where Tagore wrote, the cozy English street where Shakespeare grew up, the bars where Hemingway drank.

"Books have been my only connection with the outside world that hasn't involved pain," Damini had said, when he showed her pictures of his travels.

Damini told him everything about her life. Things she'd

never shared with anyone. About her mother, her sister who could capture a person's dying breath, her journey of being in constant pain and, for the first time in her life, the kind of life she really wanted.

She had seen Amrit first thing this morning at the hospital and told him about the power of the honey moon. His response had made her laugh. "Go to your *honey moon* tonight so we can go on our *honeymoon* soon." Then, he took a moment and, completely out of tune, sang her his favorite song: "Pal pal dil ke pas, tum rehti ho." Every moment you are close to my heart.

Damini walks faster, trying to navigate a way through a busy shopping district. She catches her reflection on the glass door of a clothing store and stops for a moment. She can't remember the last time she looked so happy, so filled with joy and anticipation. To be at the cusp of freedom was a privilege not granted to beings like her. Her sister, Yamini, for instance, bore the eternal curse of being a blessing. Yamini, a gifted healer, was unlike anyone else in Damini's family. While the heavens had gifted the rest of them a choice, no one knew why there was no way out for Yamini. None that they were aware of, anyway.

As a child, Damini looked up to Yamini. She was ethereal, soft-spoken, and seemed to glide when she walked. Yamini's smile soothed, her touch relieved, and her voice calmed even the most agitated soul. The sisters, scouring old Vedic texts, had found a way out for Damini. But despite years of researching, nothing had shown up that could release Yamini.

"No one can help me. I don't know how to tell you this, but I almost killed a man—a hospice guard—to keep my power a secret. There is no way out for me now. I will live forever like this." Yamini had wept when the sisters spoke a few days ago.

But now, Damini smiles. She knows there is a way out for her, and soon she will find the way out for her sister. As Amrit reminded her, "The great Hafiz says there is a way out through the cup of love. She will find her way out through love." Damini hadn't exactly understood what he meant, but nevertheless she believed him.

She begins to run as she feels Nisha's pain reaching her heart. The pain comes in jolts and pierces her sides, shocks her system. But Damini isn't worried. She is close to the Pool of the Weeping Lotus. That's where this pain will leave her forever.

She had asked him one night, "You know, Amrit. I take on the pain of the acid attack, the butchered arm, the gangrene-infected leg, the smashed skull, yet most days, I want a life where the most exciting point of my day is winning a bargaining war with the vegetable vendor. I want babies to spoil, a garden with flowers that bloom and die. I want to drape myself in chiffons and silks. I want to be terrified watching a scary movie and cry my eyes out at a romantic one. Does that make me selfish?" His response had made her feel confident in her decision.

"It is called wanting to be human. Why should you not be given what you want?"

A car whizzes by, splashing Damini with rainwater from the streets. She wonders if the driver is oblivious to her presence, or perhaps he sees her too late, a lady in white, and is mortified, too afraid to slow down. Or, like many unenlightened humans she knows, unaware of anything outside his own little bubble. She laughs to herself at the irony of the thought: Isn't this what I am seeking to become—an unenlightened human being?

She begins to laugh out loud as the splashed water feels like a cleansing. Her thoughts are liberating.

Damini reaches the Pool of the Weeping Lotus. Her first destination of the night.

The moon is directly over the pond. Several of the lotus flowers are snuggled on the gentle waterbed. They are closed, asleep in the quiet of the night as they wait for her to bring them strength and power to open and glow again in the morning sun. The weeping lotus, filled with the pain she gives it, is said to be the cure for the madness that haunts many. The people who know come in the mornings to gather these flowers. They crush the petals and make a paste. That paste is given to those who can't live without the doses of bhang, the sniffs of coke, the needles of heroin. The petals take the addiction away and bring peace to the addicts. The cycle of pain to peace through petals; that is what Damini really offers the world.

The air is cool. The veil between the worlds is thinner and easier to penetrate at this time of night. Damini shivers a little as the breeze envelopes her water-soaked kaftan.

As always, she does a check of the surroundings making sure there is no one around

Almost ritualistically, she checks her phone. There is only one message that had come in earlier from Yamini: *IT IS YOUR NIGHT. BE FREE, MY SISTER. BE FREE. I LOVE YOU. AND I WOULD LIE IF I SAID THAT I DIDN'T ENVY YOU THIS NIGHT.*

Believe, Yamini. Remember when Mother told us about the poet Rumi? Your salvation is seeking you. I promise.

There are no other calls, no messages.

The pond is large, about the size of a cricket field. It's

surrounded by red bricks and filled with lotuses of every possible color under the sun. Of course, at night, they all look the same. *Night is the great equalizer for the lotus flowers, just as pain is the great equalizer for humans*, Damini thinks as she sits down on top of the bricks. Her heart has started to throb with the pain now. It's beginning to sear her insides.

"I just can't imagine . . . if it hurts me so much, how much would it have hurt that poor young woman and that old security guard?" she whispers to the flowers.

Damini closes her eyes and calls on her spirit to release the evil of this wretched world. She moves forward, bends, and places her hands gently into the water.

"Sparsh, touch. Sparsh, touch. Svikroti, accept. Svikroti, accept." Damini prays to the waters to accept her touch and to grant her the blessing of accepting the pain.

A slim, glittering silver light blazes from her fingers. It sizzles through the water and towards the roots of the lotus, deep, deep inside the pond. Her heart continues to throb. She slows her breathing and begins a mantra.

"The Weeping Lotus Heals. The Weeping Lotus Heals . . ."

The Weeping Lotus accepts her earnest chants and welcomes her in.

As is always the case at this point of the transfer process, Damini can no longer feel her body, the air, or any part of this world. She hears nothing. She sees nothing. She feels nothing. She is now inside herself and one with the pain and with the healing.

The silver light twinkles and then disappears. The water takes on the red color of the blood that begins to leave Damini's fingers and drip into the pond. Drip, drop, drip, drop, the tiny droplets leave her, taking the pain with them. Drip, drop, drip, drop, the essence of the burning flesh plunges into the deep, calm waters.

This is the one precious moment that Damini loves. The one moment where she feels like a part of something bigger than her pain, the part that shows that she, like any other person on this planet, is a part of a larger spirit. The water in the pond begins to glow gently and then it happens, the closed lotus flowers open up and flickers of light emanate from their core. The flowers glow for a few, beautiful, mesmerizing seconds.

Then they close. They have what they need. Tomorrow, they will be plucked and they will be the antidote to someone else's pain. Damini smiles. She will miss this part of her life. But, she reminds herself, it's for good reason. After all, isn't love the most powerful pain killer of all?

Her fingers are no longer bleeding. Her heart no longer hurts.

Usually at this point, she's exhausted and sleeps the night away in her tiny little hut next to the pond, but tonight she gets up with renewed energy and spirit. She bows to the pond, thanking it for all its help, assuring it that there will be others who will come and release their pain into the pond, and the pain-to-peace cycle will never be broken.

She bows again with respect and rushes to her final destination: The Garden of Harmony. The moon glows sweetly and guides her path in the dark. The Garden is a mere one hundred and eight steps away. Damini had counted a few weeks ago. Just like the one hundred and eight beads in her mala. Odd coincidence. Or was it?

She rushes, needing to get there in time, her footsteps the only sound in the dark. While she has lived just outside the Garden of Harmony her whole life, Damini has never dared to go inside.

She comes upon what appears to be a dead end.

In front of her are three large, thorny rose bushes. She panics. What now?

She looks up at Chand, the moon god. "Show me the way. If I am true to you, and if I have fulfilled my mission, show me the way to my freedom."

Nothing happens for a moment. But Damini stays steady. Folding her hands in prayer, repeating her heartfelt request to the powers that be.

Then she notices a moonbeam dancing under one of the rose bushes. There is a pathway that leads straight into the garden.

Damini gets on her knees and crawls into the bush.

The thorns pierce her back, hands, knees, and arms.

She winces, but no thorns can keep her away from her destiny.

A little bit of pain for a lifetime of peace.

It's so dark Damini can't see anything when she comes out of the thorn-infested tunnel. The moon is suddenly covered by clouds and there's no other light.

Damini feels her body tense, and she shivers at the darkness. It feels like a vacuum. No sight, no sound, nothing to feel, to reassure Damini that she is in the right place and at the right time.

What if this was a charade? What if I will never be normal? What if I am like Yamini and cursed to bear this brunt forever? Damini thinks as she pulls thorns out of her flesh.

Damini stands up and shakes herself. This isn't the time for doubt. The Garden doesn't take kindly to the ones who don't believe.

As if on cue, suddenly there is a loud, piercing sound.

Damini is startled for a second, but then realizes the sound is her phone. Here, the noise tears through the silence.

She wonders what to do.

If she answers, and it's someone in pain, she is duty-bound to go and help.

She looks at her phone and recognizes the number. The caller hangs up and sends a text message. *THANK YOU AGAIN FOR TONIGHT. I OWE YOU. AND, OH, WERE YOU ABLE TO MAKE CONTACT?*

YOUR WORK WILL BE DONE. I PROMISE, Damini types back.

She puts the phone away and then folds her hand in prayer.

"Thank you, Chand, I am ready now. I want to marry Amrit. I want to have babies. I want to live a normal life. I have done things for others for centuries and tonight ask for mercy. For the biggest blessing of all. I ask, humbly, for my life to be mine. To live as I please."

The clouds clear away and the garden glows under the radiance of the honey moon.

The beautiful garden is filled with golden flowers. In the center there is a statue of Soma, the elixir goddess known to relieve pain.

Damini walks up to the statue and gets down on her knees.

This is it.

Her moment has arrived.

She closes her eyes and speaks from her heart:

I am free of guilt, I am free of angst.

I am full of love.

I have served my purpose.

I have answered every person in need.

I am free of guilt, I am complete.

I have done all that was expected of me.

Soma, relieve me of my duties. Give me the elixir of life as a human. To be free.

To have free will.

To have a life without pain.

Damini feels a calm settle in. Breathing comes easier, feels effortless. She feels weightless. She opens her eyes and looks up at the statue of Goddess Soma, her heart filled with hope. Tears begin to flow as she thanks the goddess accepting her prayers.

She closes her eyes again. Her arms are out in front, waiting to receive the final blessing from Goddess Soma.

I release my power of pain.

I release my power of pain.

I release my power of pain.

She closes her eyes as a deep peace descends upon her body.

Damini begins to feel the same way she does healing someone—as pain comes into her system, she feels her heart tighten, limbs like someone is slicing them. Her fingers turn blue as the blood circulation stops. She tries to open her mouth to scream, but no words come. She can't move. This is the worst pain she has ever experienced—like a thousand gallons of acid have been thrown on her tiny body. Like a steamroller has just crushed her under its weight.

She keeps repeating the chant in her heart, trying to block out the pain.

I release my power of pain.

I release my power of pain.

The clouds hide the moon and it's dark again.

A single cell at a time, the powerful pain begins to leave. Excruciatingly slowly. If she stops her chant, the pain returns with a vengeance. It is testing her endurance. Mocking her. As if asking: How badly do you want to be free?

I release my power of pain.

I release my power of pain.

A million times over. Maybe more. She continues to chant, undeterred, strong. Believing.

Damini feels the warmth returning to her hands, her feet.

She moves her fingers. The pain is slipping away. She feels her breath becoming steady and a joy in her spirit that she has never felt before. She touches her chest. That special part that holds the pouch that stores the pain she gathers. It often bulges to remind Damini of who she is. It is gone. She touches it again. Gone. There's nothing there.

She allows herself a smile. A big broad smile. She bows to Goddess Soma. She looks up and blows kisses to Chand, the moon god.

She stands and steadies herself. She looks at her hands, her arms, her legs and moves her limbs, ever so slightly. There is no pain. Nothing. She is free. She is truly and completely free.

She twirls in her kaftan, giggling like a little girl. Laughing, smiling, now blowing many kisses to the god and goddess. To the Garden, to the pond, to the ones she helped and to the ones she can't.

Dear ones who will have pain: Find it in your heart to forgive me for not being able to help. My duty is over. I pray you will find someone who heals you well. Bless me on this new path and my chosen journey now.

She is giddy with joy.

She takes out her phone to call Amrit. But before she can, her phone rings. She looks at the number. It's the hospital. They only call when they need her services.

She debates what to do. *At this point, I can help no one. I'm a free soul now. Not bound to anyone or anything. Except my love, Amrit,* she says to herself.

She answers the phone.

"Damini, this side," she says as she touches her chest again to make sure the pain pouch is gone. Yes, it's gone. There is nothing there except her beating heart.

She stares up and blows yet another kiss towards the honey moon.

"Damini, it's Sister Angela. I'm sorry to let you know that Amrit passed away a few minutes ago. I didn't want you to hear it from anyone else. Heart attack. I am so sorry."

The Truth Often Lies

Sister Angela's story

Sister Angela just lied. Blatantly. And seemingly with no regard for consequences.

"You are a nun. How could you do this to me? How could you tell Damini I am dead?" Amrit is seated on his hospital bed. Anger makes his frail body shudder. He tries to shift a little to see if he can get a bit more comfortable, but that seems to be impossible today. Even the slightest move causes sharp pain. He stops fidgeting and stares at Sister Angela, waiting for her answer. Damini is the love of his life and now, thanks to this unethical woman, dressed in a gentle gray habit, the love of his life thinks he is dead. "How could you? On the day that is most important to her. How could you do this to her? To me. To us. I thought you cared for us, Sister Angela."

"Amrit, forgive me. Damini's gift helps so many people. Her powers are a huge blessing. Even you—you would have died of sheer agony had she not come and helped you. You want to deny the rest of the world that? Why? Now that she thinks you are dead, she won't go through the ritual to give up her power. We need her power to help so many. I know you hate me, but I did the right thing." Sister Angela's eyes are filled with indignation.

She stands at the edge of his bed, hands on her side.

"Oh, really? Then why can't you look me in the eye and tell me. Tell me, Amrit, she can never have the normal life she so craves—the marriage, the babies. You took her choice away. Tell me again, how that is the right thing. Look me in the eye."

"Amrit, the world needs Damini to do her duty."

Amrit shakes his head. "You have no right to do what you just did. This special moon, the honey moon, comes only once every one hundred years. Now she has to bear other people's pain for another century."

"Amrit, this isn't about you and her, or me. Her ability to take away pain is needed too much." Sister Angela's tone is softer, kinder, and gentler as she looks at the forlorn man.

"Now, we'll never be able to get married. She will be a prisoner forever," Amrit says as a lone tear trickles down his cheek.

Sister Angela adjusts her habit and then sits down on the bed by Amrit's feet.

"These blessings or burdens are not ours to give away. We are given these for a reason and, in her case, she is a blessing to everyone she meets. How do you think she will feel the next time she meets someone in real pain and can't help them? Would that be a good feeling?" Sister Angela knows she's fighting a battle already won. This discussion is moot at this point. She believes she stopped Damini from going through the ritual and that is all that counts.

"I guess I was being selfish. I fell in love with her. I am and always will be in love with her. I just want to spend the rest of my life with her," Amrit says, as he lies back down on the bed and pulls a thin blanket over his head.

Sister Angela debates what to do. She was called in just a couple of hours ago, because Amrit had complained to the staff that he was having sharp pains and feeling uneasy. He'd asked for Damini. The nurse on duty couldn't get in touch with Damini, so she called Sister Angela. As Sister Angela comforted him and checked his vitals, Amrit told her what Damini was going to do. Almost immediately, she picked up the phone and without hesitation told Damini that Amrit was dead. But there was more. Something she has to share with Amrit.

"Amrit, also . . . I—" Sister Angela wants to tell him an important truth, but he isn't going to believe her, especially since she just blatantly lied in front of him.

The truth is never as simple as it seems.

Here she is, calling herself Sister Angela, but she has never set foot in a convent, never been ordained. She did what she needed to survive. *People think lying is complicated. They should try telling the truth.*

Sister Angela decides not to say anything. She stands up, straightens her habit, wishes him well, and focuses her energy on the next task at hand.

This is how it always ends for Sister Angela—getting always blamed for happenings she has no power over; blamed for what the Divine, if you can call it that, makes her do. But she always reasons that everyone has their load to carry. Damini has hers, Angela has hers, and Amrit certainly has his.

***

Sister Angela's gift—or nightmare, depending on the day—was first discovered when she was about five years old. From what little she remembered about that time, she'd had a tranquil, carefree childhood, a humble home, and every day hot meals to eat, turmeric-hued milk to drink, and a soft bed to sleep in.

Angela's small, brightly painted orange house was nestled in the hills of Dronanagri. Perpetual blue skies, soft gentle breezes, cool nights, and magnificent springs made this city a paradise for its residents and a tourist magnet for people tired of choking on pollution in the surrounding larger cities. One of little Angela's favorite spots was the Buddha temple with its hundred stupas. The golden Buddha statue, over a hundred feet tall and gleaming in the Dronanagri sun, always made Angela happy.

"Mama, looking at this makes it feel like flowers are blooming in my heart."

Her mother carried her from stupa to stupa so that the young girl could touch and roll them. She was tiny and couldn't reach the black, mantra-inscribed stupas on her own. If her mother got tired, which she often did, Angela would charm one of the young lamas into carrying her. Each time she touched a stupa, she would clap with glee.

"Such joy," one of the young lamas remarked once, "radiates only from ones connected to divinity."

Nothing was expected of Angela and that made life idyllic. When she was especially good, her mother fed her hisalu, the tiny golden Himalayan raspberries. "These little berries protect your heart," her mother would tell her. Some mornings, her mom would slice open tiny pieces of kaphal, a sour dried raspberry, and sprinkle it with chili and salt. Angela much preferred the sweeter hisalu, but her mom insisted that she needed to eat both for optimum health. Her mother made a living selling jams and jellies of these local berries. The tourists loved them, and even the locals took to them.

Then, just as a dark cloud sometimes appears out of the nowhere on a sunny day, her life changed when Angela began asking her mother strange questions.

"Mama, why does that man have a dark stain on his face? Mama, why does that little girl have a black mark on her knees?"

"I don't see anything, child. Where are you seeing black marks?" Her mother became increasingly frustrated.

Finally, at the prodding of an older relative, her mother took Angela to see a local pediatrician. "I don't know what's wrong with her. She keeps telling me she sees black marks on people. The eye doctor, you know the one behind the deer park? He checked her out, and there's nothing wrong with her eyes. I even took her to another eye doctor on the other side of the valley. He's married to my cousin and studied in America. He didn't take any fees and said her eyes are fine."

"Angela, do you see a black mark on me?" the doctor asked gently.

She stared at him for a minute, then pointed to his heart.

The doctor appeared flustered and Angela's mother sensed it and panicked.

"What is it? What is *wrong* with Angela?"

The doctor, Angela recalled, had pulled out a prescription pad and written something, and handed it to Angela's mother. It would be years before Angela could read it. *Please do not show any emotion as I do not want to scare your beautiful daughter. Bear with me as I conduct a quick experiment.*

The kind doctor had taken her by the hand and whispered,

"I'm going to take you to a special room and I want you to point out any child you see with a dark black stain or mark, as you say, okay? Then, if you feel like you can tell me—and just me—show where the stain is."

His demeanor calmed Angela, but she recollected her mother seeming anxious.

"What is wrong with her, doctor? Where are you taking Angela?" Her mother had tried to pull the child away from the doctor's grip.

"There is nothing wrong with her. I just want to test a theory," he'd said.

Angela's mother had let go and the doctor took Angela into the waiting room of the clinic. He prompted her to point to the children and tell him, quietly, what she saw. She began to point and whisper.

The doctor showed no emotion, just took notes on a piece of paper.

He had then taken Angela back to her mother in the examination room, shut the door, and rubbed his forehead. What he had witnessed went against everything his science background had taught him.

"Mrs. Geen, your daughter is special."

Mrs. Geen stood quiet and still. *Special* was not a label anyone in these parts wanted associated with daughters. Boys could be special and unique. Girls needed only to be homely and quiet.

"I don't know if you have ever heard that an animal, say, a dog, can sense illness, like cancer or an oncoming stroke in a person. Of course, they do it by smell. But your little girl, she does it by sight. I think she sees illnesses." The doctor chose his words carefully. "She is a miracle of sorts and I would love to have her meet other doctors and do some research to find out how her brain works. She could revolutionize medicine."

Mrs. Geen looked bewildered.

As simply as he could, the doctor explained that Angela had correctly pointed out every sick child in the room, and specifically to the part of their body that was affected. The doctor knew Angela was correct, as most of these were his regular patients. Even more so, earlier in his exam room, she had correctly pointed to his heart as being sick. He had recently received a pacemaker and there was no way for this five-year-old to know that.

Angela couldn't understand what all the fuss was about. She wanted to go out and play and have a vanilla softy with her friends. This wasn't how she liked spending her afternoon—she wasn't sick, so why was she in this silly doctor's office?

"Mama, I just want to go home."

Her mama had picked Angela up and hugged her.

"Mama has no dark parts," Angela said, holding onto her mother for dear life.

Mrs. Geen put Angela back down on the floor.

"Doctor, I don't know what this means. Will she have a normal life?"

The doctor bent and kissed Angela's forehead. "She is the angel of mercy. She can see what no mortal can and this gives her a superpower: a method of prophetic healing."

That was the beginning of the end of her childhood. At first, Mrs. Geen was happy when Angela could point to a relative's arm and tell them the arm was sick and to get it checked. Lots of people came for free advice. It seemed like all was well.

But then her business took a hit. The harvest was poor and making the jellies became impossible. Mrs. Geen confided in a local neighbor, a man called Jags, "I have no man in my life and no way to make money now. I don't know what to do." The business-minded Jags came up with an easy solution: charge for Angela's superpowers, commercialize the talent instead of giving away free prophetic healing.

Mrs. Geen thought it was a marvelous idea. She took Angela to the tourist spots: they sat outside the deer park, or near the various temples. But people ignored them. "What rubbish! I'm not sick. You are crazy," were the typical responses.

So Mrs. Geen returned to Jags. "It isn't working. What should I do?"

"It is all a matter of marketing. Have you learned nothing from all the sadhus and yogis who line the temples?" Jags smiled, thinking, *This girl is a goldmine. One that I can cash in on as well. I just need to keep her mother close.*

No one wanted to hear from a normal little girl, so Mrs. Geen and Jags concocted a wonderful plan: Mrs. Geen stitched a tiny habit with a dark veil, and Angela, now six, became Sister Angela.

Little Sister Angela would sit on the veranda of their tiny house and hold health court. At first it was for an hour a day, as people were unsure she could actually see or diagnose anything. But then word spread. Eventually she sat for six hours a day. Every day. It was a gift from God, Mrs. Geen would say. They didn't even need to leave the house and the money was rolling in. Jags did his part by bringing in the tourists. His business, driving a tour bus, tripled as more and more tourists came in wanting to see Sister Angela before doing anything any else.

For Angela it meant no school, no friends, no music, no TV, no games, no dancing in the rain, no singing in the sunshine. Day in and day out, she saw black spots and pointed to them.

Angela protested. She hated sitting there. She hated constantly seeing sick people. She hated, even more, those who insisted that they *were* sick but that she was too stupid to see their illness. When she cried, she was given chocolates as a treat. When she got up to try to leave, Mrs. Gee had no choice, as she told Jags, but to beat the child into submission, at one point even chaining Angela to the chair. Angela quickly learned that protesting just made things worse.

Business was booming. Mrs. Geen hired doctors to set up desks outside her house. The girl saw the area of illness, the doctor confirmed it, and Mrs. Geen and Jags, who had now left his wife and lived with Mrs. Geen, celebrated with chuwarak, a distilled pineapple alcohol that Jags stocked up on when he travelled to Tripura.

Mrs. Geen told Angela, "I love you. I hope you know that I'm doing this for the good of the people. See how many people you are helping every day? You are God's own child!" She presented Angela with a beautiful new habit and a brand new area for sitting, with more comfortable chairs, shoes, and a supply of Angela's favorite foods—sweet drinks, potato chips, chocolates, and cakes. It was Angela's sixteenth birthday and she had gone from a beautiful, slight girl to a quiet, depressed teen.

One day, she announced, "I don't want to do this today. I want to go out and have friends and adventures. I don't want to wear this habit. Just today, Mother." Angela, now taller than her mother, begged and pleaded.

"Look at the line. People have come from all over the world. They are now paying six times the price we used to get. You can't just leave."

"Mother, I'm sick of sick people. I can't eat or sleep, all I see are black circles everywhere. Please, just today?" For the first time ever, Angela stomped out of the house. *It is all too much. I can't do this anymore.*

"Angela, how dare you! You come back here *now*," Mrs. Geen screamed and screamed, but Angela was gone. Mrs. Geen quickly found Jags. Something needed to be done.

And that something came in the form of Merlin.

Merlin, with her doe-eyes, short brown hair, high-pitched laugh, innumerable Sanskrit shlokas tattooed on her arms, and quirky sense of humor, was brought in by Jags to be Angela's keeper. Mrs. Geen and Jags were now starting to travel and spend all the money that just kept flowing in, and someone needed to keep Angela motivated and going.

Angela liked Merlin instantly. Merlin was everything Angela wanted to be: free-spirited, optimistic, and totally high on life. Merlin encouraged Angela, showing her constantly how her skills helped real people in need. Those who had gone to every doctor they could find but had no diagnosis. Those who couldn't afford to go to a doctor.

"You are a gift for these people. You may see hundreds of them, but they only have one of you." Merlin's words began to soothe Angela and she started to settle in her role.

They made it a game. If Angela got through more than twenty people in an hour, Merlin would take her to the Buddha temple. If she got through thirty, they would go to the Tapkeshwar Temple and watch the drops of water disappear into the earth. A gentle friendship blossomed. Mrs. Geen and Jags were delighted. Their earnings had doubled since Merlin came in.

Then, one evening, Merlin took Angela to the one place that Angela had wanted to go but never been. She took Angela to the thousand-fold spring on the banks of the river Kali Gad. The two went in to take a dip. The gandhak jal, the water that smelled of sulphur, soothed their spirits. The girls splashed around, acting like children, and even chatted with the tourists. Then, just as they were ready to step out of the water, Merlin turned to Angela, held her face in her hands, and kissed her on the lips.

That memory still made Sister Angela's eyes fill with tears.

***

"Sister Angela, is all well?" A nurse stuck her head into Amrit's room. Sister Angela was standing there, lost in sad thought.

"Yes, I was just leaving," Sister Angela nodded. She closed her eyes and said a blessing over Amrit. *Nowhere does it say only a holy man or woman can bless someone*, she thought. The sun would be up soon and she decided to go back home. There was nothing more to be done at the hospital.

As she stepped out, she remembered that kiss. The softness of Merlin's lips. The safety she felt in her arms. Their lovemaking was natural and beautiful. After that day, Angela went through the patients as quickly as she could so she and Merlin could be alone together.

***

On the night of her twentieth birthday, Angela invited Merlin to her room to celebrate. Neither one heard Mrs. Geen and Jags come in. The couple saw the girls in their romantic embrace.

The next day, Jags gave Merlin a check for more money than she could imagine and told her to leave and never to return. He took away her phone.

Angela kept asking her mother where Merlin had gone and was told that Merlin had a family emergency.

"She would never leave me without telling me, Mother. What have you done?" Angela's eyes blazed with anger. But there was no response. Her mother insisted that Angela go back to her duties. The lines outside were long.

Angela kept calling Merlin's phone, but there was no response. Jags, clearly irritated with Angela's lack of focus on the customers, took away *her* phone now.

Later that day, while her mother and Jags were negotiating the rate with a new load of tourists, Angela slipped out of her house to try and find Merlin. She looked everywhere Merlin had taken her, but there was no sign of her friend.

Angela didn't want to go back home. Instead, she found solace on the streets of her hometown, sleeping under trees, inside boxes, eating at the free meal stations set up at the temples. She revisited every single place that she and Merlin had ever been, hoping to find her again. She wept, she begged the Universe, she prayed, but there was no trace of Merlin.

Perhaps, she reasoned, some things are just not meant to be.

Her one consolation was that she hadn't worn the veil or consulted in a week, and it was freeing. She could just be Angela, a normal young woman with nothing special to offer. And it was the most liberating feeling in the world. She kept wandering the streets during the day, hiding inside temples or the local caves at night.

A week later, LOST WOMAN posters with Angela's face began popping up around the city. Angela laughed at the irony. When Sister Angela held health court, her mother had insisted she wear a veil to "look the part," so no one really knew what Angela looked like. Now, to disappear, she simply donned her veil again and became invisible.

Also, as advised by Merlin and unbeknownst to her mother, Angela had frequently taken handfuls of cash from the box that her mother used to gather donations, and hidden it in her room in a golden box. The day she left, she had buried the box in the backyard.

When the posters went up, Angela knew her time in the valley was over. She went back to her house in the middle of the night, got the money box, and checked into a local hotel. She planned to leave the valley, but wanted to stay one more night in the hopes of finding Merlin. She wandered the streets that night, asking everyone she ran into if they had seen Merlin. But everyone said no.

The next morning, before Angela left her beloved city, she went to take a dip in the healing, gandhak jal waters of Sahastradhara. She took off her shoes and stepped into the spring water. She kept walking until the water was over her head and she was completely enveloped by the healing liquid. When she popped her head back out, she saw a familiar face on the banks of the river, waving wildly.

Angela and Merlin took the night train to Shahajahanabad, never to return.

In the new city, they rented a small room near a government-run hospital. They spent a few days getting set up. Merlin began to teach dance classes and, on her own accord, Angela began to visit the hospital in her habit to talk to those who were sick. She never pointed out any dark spots or called attention to her skills. She just talked to people and tried to be a friend—something she had never had the chance to do. She would casually focus their energy on their "hurt" and then ask them to release it. Some of the doctors suspected Sister Angela knew a lot more than she let on, but no one said anything. She came and went as she pleased, as a messenger of God, and most patients loved her visits. Finally, Angela found peace with her calling.

***

That is how things had been with Amrit. He used to love having her visit him.

After having Sister Angela see him at least a dozen times, the staff was happy to report that Amrit was getting better. His crush on Damini had become the talk of the hospital staff.

"Two of the sweetest people to get together, don't you think?" Nurse Madhuja, one of the senior nurses on staff, had confided in Sister Angela. Angela had nodded knowingly. Having Merlin in her life was the greatest gift from the Divine.

Sister Angela had been thrilled at the prospect of Damini and Amrit getting together. Her visits to Amrit had been different than to other patients. While most only wanted to talk about their illness or have her pray for them, or have her ask God why He was being so cruel to them, Amrit was different. He would recite poetry from his old journal and read to Sister Angela the works of Tagore in his most distinguished voice. It was as though the words were his saviors. His voice would make the words come alive, his eyes would glitter, his hands would gesture, and his whole being became one with the words. His clean aura glowed and she was thrilled the young man had fought his cancer and won his life back.

It was a week or so ago that Damini had confided in Sister Angela about the upcoming honey moon and its significance, and how she could use it to end her cycle of pain. Sister Angela had listened with a bittersweet feeling clutching at her heart. *I would do anything to get rid of my own cursed blessing*, she thought.

"You should do this. I would normally not be supportive as your blessing helps so many, but you have the love of your life waiting, you have the potential to lead a normal life. Go, Damini, go and do this," had been Sister Angela's final words to Damini.

Yet so much can change, so fast. This morning had started out like any other. Sister Angela got ready to visit the hospital, and Amrit in particular. She remembered this night would be the big night—the night of the honey moon, the time Damini would be free. Despite the tinge of envy in her heart, Sister Angela had smiled and said a prayer for Amrit and Damini, and even for herself, as she made her way to the hospital.

After doing her rounds with other patients, Sister Angela stopped by Nurse Madhuja's desk. They had established a lovely kinship, and Nurse Madhuja always had kind words for Sister Angela. They spent their precious few minutes together discussing Amrit and Damini, and the possible upcoming nuptials. Then Madhuja had to leave to attend to her duties.

Sister Angela was done with her regular visits and had been thrilled to go and see Amrit. She had even called Merlin to share the news with her. "I will plan all the dances for the wedding!" Merlin was jubilant.

The busy hospital, as usual, was filled with the sick, but today she wasn't having any of that. She refused to look at anyone, keeping her eyes focused on the floor as she managed to squeeze through the crowd to Amrit's room.

She knocked on the door.

"Come in, come in. I am bored to tears," had been the familiar and sweet response.

Sister Angela remembered how happy she had been to hear his voice, and she'd smiled and opened the door. She entered and looked at Amrit and wanted to congratulate him, to tell him this was going to be the best day of his life.

Then she saw them: the deep, deep, dark black spots that covered most of his head, the dark spots she saw through the bandages, inside his skull. The dark spots of death.

Angela knew then she had to make a call to stop Damini. Amrit was going to need her pain killer skills now more than ever. And, Angela thought, no point in two lives being destroyed in one night.

The Keeper of Lost Memories

Nurse Madhuja's story

Nurse Madhuja didn't hate that Sister Angela had lied, because she felt she would have done the same thing: sacrifice the one for the cause of the tribe. She and Sister Angela shared a close relationship and both understood that the decisions they made were not easy or kind. Deep in her heart, she couldn't even begin to fathom the depth of sorrow that must have hit Amrit.

"It's his burden to bear," Sister Angela had argued. Indeed, thought Madhuja, it was.

The following morning Madhuja had been fielding calls on Amrit's phone. There were several calls from some woman named Yamini asking for her sister, Damini. Yamini was worried that Damini wasn't answering her phone, and wanted to see if Amrit knew what was going on.

Amrit, heartbroken, refused to take the calls, and all Madhuja could do was to tell her to keep trying to call Damini.

"You don't understand. She went to a . . . a secret place yesterday and now, she isn't answering my calls. I'm worried something happened to her." Yamini was clearly upset and concerned.

"I don't know anything." Madhuja was a bad liar and her tone gave her away.

"Please, I beg you. Tell me. Is she alive?"

As calmly as she could, Madhuja related the events of the previous night. Yamini just listened and then hung up without saying a word.

Amrit—what was left of him physically—was curled up into a ball, shrinking away from the world.

Madhuja brushes off all thoughts of Amrit and Damini and busies herself with paperwork at the hospital. She begins to go through the files one at a time, meticulously, slowly reading each page, correcting, making sure all the paperwork is in order. She hates this part of her job, but it's the only way she can stay at the hospital without having a nursing degree. Of course, no one here suspects anything, yet. The hospital had no need to suspect she lied on her forms.

Nurse Madhuja has been at the hospital for over ten years now, but not as a nurse. Her excuse—a nasty back injury certified by a well-known doctor—has allowed her to be permanently bound to a desk job. Just as she desires.

For those ten years, she had kept her secret. Most people treat her as they do women of great beauty: with understated disdain, assuming she must be arrogant as all beauties are. And that suited Madhuja just fine. Of course, some were kinder than others, but Madhuja kept her distance.

All they knew—all she told them—was that she was a very capable woman who didn't want to be a practicing nurse anymore, but could handle more paperwork than their entire nursing staff put together. She had fake certificates and recommendations to prove it. The head of this private hospital, an old man in a wheelchair, understood what it was like to have a broken back and gave her a desk job. She filed paperwork, quietly, efficiently, and peacefully. She kept to herself, for the most part—except for Sister Angela.

On one particularly bad night, when she saw the worst humanity had to offer, she drank almost three glasses of whiskey. She wasn't a drinker and the alcohol went straight to her head. She dialed the only person she knew would understand what it meant to be different: Sister Angela. While Sister Angela had a love-hate relationship with her gift, Madhuja couldn't be happier with hers.

"It's always like this, right? One man's food is another man's poison," she had said to Sister Angela.

Madhuja, a nurse to everyone around her, had been born in the deep and dark mangrove forests of the Sundarbans, on the delta of three most magnificent rivers. Madhuja's earliest memory was of a couple whom she called her parents, taking her regularly to the heart of the forest and setting her down in front of a wall. She remembered they prayed once a month at the foot of the impossibly large, looming dark wall. They would evoke the great Bon Bibi, worshipped by people of all religions, before entering the forest, because she protected them from the savage tigers. Bon Bibi was brought all the way from the dual kingdoms of Hejaz and Najd. Madhuja couldn't understand their words as they muttered, though. After their muttering, they would turn to look at her as if to see a reaction. She would simply smile. Then they would shake their heads and take her home again. And oh, how she loved that home. Nestled in the deep woods, their home was surrounded by tigers, deer, and the occasional crocodile. Her parents seemed more at home with the animals than they did with other humans. Madhuja grew up hand-feeding baby cubs, cuddling does, and working with her parents to collect honey. One night they told her that her name, Madhuja, meant "made of honey"—as that was how sweet she was.

The honey they collected with the comb, and mixed with a mysterious pollen-like ingredient they would add once they got it back home, sold for the price of something called "gold." Although young Madhuja didn't know what gold meant, she understood it must have been precious as it brought in amazing prosperity. First, the hut was converted into a house, then they got a magical button that brought in light during the night and moved air in the house on hot days. One special evening, her parents bought a box that sang beautiful songs when you pressed a button.

The trio was happy. The only time there was uneasiness was at the wall. The crying wall.

They took great precautions to reach it, praying to Bon Bibi to keep them safe and even offering additional prayers to Bon Bibi's arch enemy, Dokhin Rai, a Brahmin sage, so that the two of them together could protect the family from the creatures that roamed the deep jungle. The wall was *just* a wall, until her parents started muttering. Then water would begin to drip from the crevices, the drips would turn to drops, and then suddenly the wall would be covered in sheaths of water, forming a smooth, slick screen. Madhuja never understood the point and never asked.

One night, she was awakened by a voice calling her. She began to chase the sound, running after it. It sounded familiar.

It sounded like home. Soon she found herself at the base of the wall. The wall began to cry and then she saw it. She saw her reflection in the water. She saw a woman placing her there as a baby, and her new parents finding her. Madhuja saw her own image: a waif, as thin as a petal, painted with the colors of the rainbow. She was so mesmerized by the colors she didn't hear her parents arrive.

Upon seeing her images on the wall, they fell to their knees. "You are the one. You are the keeper. We knew it when we saw your eyes. You are the keeper of lost memories—" Madhuja didn't understand and they felt it was too dangerous to keep her there to explain. "You cannot stay here anymore. The wall has given the sign. You have to go and find your purpose," they had said to her.

Madhuja had found her purpose at this hospital after years of searching and failing at most everything she tried to do.

And now, they were getting ready to promote her to the head administrative nurse position.

"Of course, it doesn't hurt that you look like a movie star," her co-workers joked.

And beautiful she is, with her violet eyes, auburn hair, flawless golden skin, and a body that came from being blessed with terrific genes. No one in the hospital has ever seen violet eyes before, and quite often there was someone at the nurses station saying, "Nurse Madhuja, please look up. I told my mother/sister/daughter/name-your-relative about your eyes and they didn't believe me. But now they can see it on their own." Madhuja always obliged with a smile and thanked them for their oohs and aahs. They wanted to know her ancestry—of course, she had to have foreign blood, as no Indian could have that eye color. They were disappointed to know she was fully Indian and that the color of her eyes and hair were just a fluke of nature.

Just as Madhuja is wrapping up the morning paperwork, she feels a tap on her shoulder. She turns around to see the orderly, Gojen, standing behind her. His face is always scrunched as though he has just eaten something sour, and the look today is no different.

"Madhuja, I need to talk to you," he says, and she closes the books. She signals him to come behind the counter so that other people won't intrude on their conversation.

"This one is bad, Madhuja. It's like someone pelted her with sharp stones. Broken bones, broken spirit, and she claims to have fallen down the stairs."

Gojen hands Madhuja a white paper slip and waits patiently. She looks around to make sure no one is looking and then gives him a money card. It's untraceable and loaded with cash. She has doubled his fee since he works so hard for her, and even more because he is trustworthy. He accepts it, looks at the card to see the amount listed, then folds his hands and bows to her.

"This is very generous of you; it will feed my parents for at least a few months. I am so grateful." He gazes fondly at her and then quickly averts his eyes so she doesn't notice. He had been secretly taking photos of her on his old phone. They are his treasure. When the whole world seemed too much, he would stare at her pictures, her intoxicating eyes, and think of her sweet laugh and gentle demeanor. His mother caught him one day, staring at her photo, and asked who it was.

"Not every love needs to be fulfilled to be whole," he told his mother.

Gojen hates taking the money from her, but his job pays next to nothing and this extra money goes a long way.

Madhuja smiles at him and then opens the folded white slip of paper:

NAME: Seema Shah (Ward 3)

AGE: 32

ADDRESS: 25 Meethi Road, Chattarpur

CHILDREN: twin girls, age two

HUSBAND: Deepak, 35, works at the bank. Very rich family. Large mansion on the farm.

OTHER PEOPLE IN HOUSE: mother-in-law, two maids, and three drivers.

Nurse Madhuja folds the note and sits back down at her desk. This is a new one.

"Can you believe this?" Gojen says, still standing beside her. She shakes her head.

"Hard to believe, but I know your information is always accurate, Gojen. I really appreciate it." She smiles at him and puts the piece of paper into a pocket.

"Please call me if you need me . . . or anything. Please." Gojen thanks her and leaves.

Madhuja watches him go. This quiet man so in love with her. She wishes she had feelings for him, but his presence just inspires warmth in her heart, not love.

She finishes her filing, locks up the cabinets and checks her pocket to make sure the paper is still there. It's lunchtime now, so the office has cleared out a bit. Just a couple of nurses joking and eating at their stations. Regardless, Madhuja looks around to make sure no one is watching and then picks up the phone.

"This is Nurse Madhuja calling from the billing office. How is the patient Seema Shah doing?" she asks the duty nurse in Ward Three.

The duty nurse whispers into the phone, "Oh, she was checked out. I tried to stop it, Nurse Madhuja, but no one listens anymore. Between you and me, I think someone is hitting her. In-laws? Husband? I've been at this job a long time and those injuries didn't come from falling down."

Just as Madhuja is about to ask another question, she hears her name.

"Madhuja, Madhuja, we must go now! It is bad." Gojen storms back into the office.

Madhuja hangs up the phone and looks at him. "What? What happened?"

"I borrowed my friend's taxi and have it ready outside. We have to go now, I will tell you in the car. The coat, take the coat." He points towards a doctor's coat hanging on the wall. She grabs it and rushes out with him.

"Nurse, is everything okay?"

Madhuja hears some of the other nurses calling out. She doesn't stop to answer. Something is terribly wrong. Gojen is never like this, and right now he's sprinting down the hall towards the parking lot where the taxis wait.

Within minutes, Gojen is inside the car at the driver's seat. Madhuja opens the front passenger door.

"No, no, you must sit in the back and pretend I am your driver," Gojen says.

Madhuja gets in the back and he speeds out of the parking lot, heading straight towards Chattarpur farms. Madhuja doesn't ask, but knows he is probably driving to where Seema Shah lives.

"What happened, Gojen?" Madhuja asks as she puts on the doctor's coat.

"I was taking out the trash near the nurses station in Ward Three and saw Seema Shah checking out against the objection of the doctor and the nursing staff."

"Yes, I know she checked out, but why the rush?"

"I left a note on the back seat. Look at who signed her out."

The silence in the car is thick, loaded with anxious energy.

"There, there, I see the house number," Gojen says, pulling in front of a pale blue bungalow with several flower-filled balconies. The bungalow has an intricate iron and wood gate. Rose vines cover the top giving it a crown of flowers.

Madhuja steps out of the car into the hot and muggy air and realizes she has forgotten the stethoscope and doctor's bag. Well, too late now.

The gate to the bungalow opens and a worried-looking young man rushes towards her.

"I just called the doctor. Did he send you? Seema refuses to go to the hospital again and now her breathing . . . well, come in and see. I'm so worried." He turns around and runs into the house signaling Madhuja to follow.

As soon as they're inside, he guides them to a bedroom. The air conditioning is running on full speed, the bedroom is ice-cold. Decorated all in pink and lavender, it looks like a little girl's room.

"Please help Seema," he says, his voice quivering with fear as he watches her labored breathing. "Doctor—I'm sorry, I don't even know your name—is she okay?" The man's eyebrows knit together as he towers over the two women on the bed.

"Mr. Shah, can you give me a few moments with your wife? I need to make sure she isn't hurt anywhere else. I would like to check her in private, unless you feel you must stay for the examination." Madhuja hopes he takes the bait.

He does.

"I'm fine, doctor. I am fine, see?" Seema tries to sit up, but the pain is too strong and she slides back down.

"Did they explain that you have three broken ribs and a punctured lung?" Madhuja asks.

"Yes, they did. I . . . well, the fall was so bad. I guess I must have been really careless. I will be careful next time," Seema says, as she winces in pain.

"Next time, you will be dead."

"Yes, yes, I must be more careful on the stairs."

Madhuja softens her gaze. *Demons haunt us all.*

"Why does she hit you?" she asks as gently as she can.

Seema stops crying and stiffens.

"No, no, whatever gave you that silly idea? My sister? Never! Reet loves me and would never do anything to hurt me. In fact, she's the one who brought me back home from the hospital, she—"

"I never said it was your sister."

"It isn't. This is none of your business. Please leave now. I need my husband."

"She will kill you. I have seen it happen before."

Seema only stares at the lotus-shaped light fixtures on the ceiling.

"Is everything okay in there? Shall I come in?" It's her

husband, Deepak. He opens the door and peeks inside.

"Give us two more minutes, she needs to check my lower back," Seema says with a faint, reassuring smile.

He nods gently and disappears behind the door.

"My sister has suffered enough. I deserve this," Seema says quietly.

Madhuja sits and listens.

"It happened when we were children. I was maybe fifteen. It was all my fault. I ruined her life. She doesn't mean to hit me. I know. She's so sorry when it happens. But the rage of that night, it lives in her. See this house? See me? I am married, Deepak loves me, She—she only has deep and terrible memories. She is broken. And it's all my fault."

Madhuja kisses the top of Seema's forehead. "From this day forward, she will never hurt you again."

Madhuja turns to leave.

"Wait, wait, what are you going to do? Don't call the police." Seema whispers so Deepak can't hear her.

Nurse Madhuja opens the door and calls out to Deepak. He's in the main living room and comes out talking on his cell phone. "That was our family doctor. He's stuck in traffic, and says he didn't send you. Who are you?" he asks sternly.

Madhuja fishes out a business card from her pocket. "I'm the head nurse from the hospital where your wife was admitted today. We were told she was serious and were worried when she checked out early. It's the new policy at the hospital to check in on our special patients."

The husband takes the card and looks at it skeptically.

"Deepak, Deepak—" Seema's voice coming from the

bedroom interrupts the conversation.

"I have to go see what she needs. What are your fees?" he asks, taking out a wallet.

"No, no fees. It's already covered. I just need to know how to reach your sister-in-law. See, she checked your wife out, but didn't sign the papers and . . . I need to get that done. Please, that will be so helpful to me." Madhuja smiles.

"What is your number? I will text it to you."

"Thanks, Mr. Shah. With any luck, your wife will never have to see the inside of a hospital again."

Just as Madhuja gets in the car, she gets a text from Sister Angela. *HAVE YOU HEARD FROM DAMINI?*

NO.

Getting in touch with Reet proves trickier than Madhuja anticipates. Reet doesn't answer. Gojen suggests sending a text message. *THIS IS J.J. HOSPITAL. WE ARE TRYING TO GET IN TOUCH WITH YOU ABOUT PAYMENT FOR SEEMA SHAH'S HOSPITAL STAY.*

"Yes, this is Reet. I paid all the damn fees," Reet calls back in an instant and speaks in a rude voice.

"Ma'am, this is serious. Your sister has made allegations against you and it's hospital policy that I have to call the police."

There is silence at the other end.

Madhuja says, "I don't *think* she's telling the truth. But it's policy so, you know, I have to call the police, but—"

"What do you want?" Reet barks into the phone.

"Ma'am, we barely make a living, as you know." Madhuja softens her voice.

"How much?"

Ah, the predictable human.

"How about thirty thousand rupees and I will forget the allegation? You can meet me at the Garden of Stillness and Sorrows this evening at nine. Oh, and ma'am, please don't call Mrs. Shah. There is nothing she can do at this point. I already have the complaint here. And, of course, I have the liberty to add to it what I want."

"You bitch. Fine. I will give you the damn money. I will deal with Seema later."

A few hours later, in her office, Madhuja prepares to leave. She looks outside the window. The evening rains are incessant, brutal, filling each crevice, hole, slit, and pothole. If the rains don't stop, the evening will be a disaster.

"I'm coming with you for this one." Gojen enters her office and stands at the entrance like a guard. He looks determined.

"Then we need to go now. It is already late. It will take an hour to get there."

They hail a taxi and head towards the garden.

The garden appears deserted. "No one with any sense will come here alone," Gojen says as he stares at the worn-down sign atop the iron gate that guards the secrets of the garden.

They walk along the gravel path. "It should be called the Garden of Blackness and Darkness, there is no color here," says Gojen, now clearly anxious.

They reach the locked gates. Madhuja tugs gently on the bronze lock and it clicks free. She gives the gate a push and it squeaks open.

They step inside and instantly feel the air is cooler. The garden, which seemed so threatening, now appears inviting.

Gojen looks around and sees rows of evenly trimmed bushes and flowers of every color.

"Oh my, this is so strange. I've never seen roses blooming along with jasmine and marigold in the same bush." He looks confused.

"Just wait here and when she shows up, tell her to come inside. I will be by that white rose bush." Madhuja begins walking towards the bushes. "Oh, and Gojen. Whatever you do, don't come behind her. Just leave."

Gojen sits down on the gravel path and waits for Reet.

"Oh, great. Thanks for this," he says as the skies open up and begin to pour on the thirsty earth. He gets up and looks around for shelter. "A garden with not a single tree. Just my luck." He goes towards the gate hoping to take shelter under the jacaranda trees outside the compound.

Then he sees her.

Reet arrives on a blue motorcycle. Her long dark hair is dripping wet, her red shirt and jeans are soaked through. She's carrying a purse, more like a pouch. She parks the bike and walks towards the garden gates.

"Nurse Madhuja asks that you meet her inside the garden near the white roses," Gojen manages to mumble as he shivers under the cold raindrops, or perhaps at the sight of this woman who seems to him to be a she-devil.

Reet stares him down and passes into the garden. "So that's her name, is it? Madhuja? Okay, let's see what games she wants to play."

Gojen notices Reet is carrying something shiny in her hand. She enters the garden, and the gate closes behind her.

He calls out, "Oh my God, she has a knife!"

The Garden of Stillness and Sorrows

Reet's story

Reet moves confidently towards the figure standing a few feet away.

The figure, who Reet assumes is that scheming Madhuja from the hospital, is standing right by the white rose bushes just as the strange man at the gate had informed her.

The rain is now strong, bitter, just like Reet likes it.

Nature is angry, as it should be.

"Madhuja? Now let's get this over with, I'm ready. Why the hell are you moving away from me?" Reet shouts into the wet night air as the figure ahead keeps moving deeper into the garden.

"I have the file. Come and get it . . . or does a little rain scare you?" the figure mocks.

"Oh, is that how this is going to be? Well, fine, have it your way." Reet waves the knife. She notices, much to her surprise, that her hands are trembling a little. She steadies herself.

The heavy downpour stops and the dark clouds disappear.

Reet stops and looks up. The sky appears apocalyptic with shades of burnt orange bleeding through the blue-black background.

"What the hell—?"

"Reet, Reet, child come, your tea is ready and your favorite fried potatoes are, too. Come eat."

Reet stands there stunned. Her body shudders. The voice. *That voice*. It can't be. That high-pitched, shrill voice belongs to her mother. Her dead mother.

"You can't trick me, Madhuja. I don't know what your plan is, but you can't trick me," Reet all but screams.

"Reet, come in from the rain. Your tea is ready. Come before it gets cold." Her mother's voice again. This time softer, closer.

"Nurse Madhuja, stop this nonsense. Just take this stupid money and give me the damn file." Reet shouts in every direction, no longer able to discern exactly where she is in the garden or the whereabouts of Madhuja. She puts a hand on her heart as if doing so will stop it from racing.

When I catch her, I will ask how she managed to get Mom's voice. She must be a witch or an insane genius. Maybe Seema helped her with this. Reet vows to take revenge on Seema for putting her in a bad situation yet again.

"Ah, Reet, you say you want to be civil and yet you have a knife? What will your mother think?" Madhuja says, letting out a shrill laugh.

"My mother is dead. You leave her out of this, you understand? Now stop this damn nonsense." Reet rushes towards the bush where the voice appears to be coming from.

She reaches the bushes and stops. The leaves are dark, almost black in color. The bushes seem taller than they did a few moments ago. Reet rubs her eyes and tries to refocus. She turns around to make sure she can still see the path, but it's dark and she can no longer differentiate the path from the grass.

The old lady's soft, sweet voice fills the garden again. "Reet, are you coming for tea? And bring that silly sister of yours as well. Seema is outside with that coconut vendor again. Why does a girl need to learn how to crack open a coconut shell? It's a useless skill and it will never help her find a husband. She needs to learn to cook like a proper wife."

Reet drops the knife, shudders and wraps her arms around herself.

The colors in the sky change from orange to dark red. The sharp wind stings Reet's skin.

Reet finds herself whispering. "What kind of a fucking joke is this, Madhuja? What game are you playing? Where is your projector hidden? Is this a TV trick? What the hell are you up to? Is Seema behind this? My dear sister, Seema? Is she here?"

She pokes around the bushes. No recorder, no device, nothing; just dirt and mulch.

"Reet, you are here."

Reet turns around and the scene unfolding takes her breath away. She sees her mother, dressed in a favorite dark yellow gown, holding a cup of tea and a plate filled with deep-fried pakoras. Reet immediately recognizes the setting: Her mother is standing in the kitchen of Reet's childhood bungalow. Her mother's hair is in a single, long braid.

"Come Reeti, my sweet child, come here, I have been waiting for you. Come in and call Seema in as well. She's been outside too long with that coconut man. What is his name again? Oh, right, Ajit. Tell him to go home now and tell her to come inside."

How could the nurse know that only her mother called her Reeti?

This has to be Seema playing games.

The air becomes thinner, cooler, and Reet starts to back away.

Beeji, my mother, is dead and gone, she thinks, again and again.

"Reeti, Seema just ate and wants you to go to the temple with her. I think she's going to fail her exams again and that bribing God will save her now."

Reet is stunned the mirage recites the exact words from that fateful day.

Reet sees her childhood friend, Yamini, seated at her mother's feet. Her mother loving, playing with Yamini's lustrous hair and teasing her. "You should be in a commercial for hair oil, or maybe that is too old-fashioned, maybe for shampoo. You have such beautiful hair."

Yamini laughs, her eyes sparkling as she tells Reet that she too will go to the temple with her and Seema.

Reet remembers that day so clearly. She remembers it clearly, because she and Seema did go to the temple that day—only it wasn't to pray; it was to meet a boy. The boy was Reet's first boyfriend. She was sixteen and Seema, a year younger, was her confidant.

Abruptly the scene with her mother, the tea, and the fried pakoras is gone.

Reet sighs, rubs her eyes, and shakes her head. There is no sound.

With nowhere else to go, Reet begins to walk on the only path visible, her legs shaking, her breathing shallow and quick. She looks around and sees the glint of the knife. Grateful for finding it, she picks it up and holds the knife close.

"Reet, is that you? I have a surprise for you. Jassie says he is coming to *propose* to you."

The dark path is illuminated with a strong green light.

Reet stops cold and stares.

It's her dead father, telling her that the boy she despised, Jassie, was planning to come over and ask for her hand in marriage.

"Bauji, is that you?" Reet asks. "Oh, what the hell am I saying? Of *course* it's not you, you're dead."

"Come sit with me, Reet." Her father is sitting in his old rattan chair, smoking his ever-present pipe, long beard flowing into his lap. His white hair runs down the length of his back. He always left his hair open after he shampooed it. He loved letting it dry in the sun.

Cautiously, she approaches the image, the mirage . . . or the reality, she isn't sure anymore.

"Bauji?" she asks. She was always his little girl. He was her hero, with his stories of slaying enemies when he was in the army, of serenading her mother even after fifty years of marriage and, of course, for showering adoration on his two daughters.

"It's such a beautiful day, Reet. Oh, this sun feels good on my skin." The voice is as she remembers; kind, filled with love, and soothing.

Reet walks towards the light and it engulfs her. She finds herself in her childhood living room, with her father seated on his chair. The sweet sounds of the mynah chirping outside, the salty smell of her mother's fried pakoras, her sister practicing her off-tune singing rather loudly in the courtyard.

She sees herself sitting at her father's feet. He pats her head gently and then speaks.

"Jassie will keep you happy, Reet. He has made much money

in selling bicycle tires. His father tells me he's driving a new imported car. He is religious and a good man."

This scene, in Reet's real life, ended with Reet agreeing to marry a man she despised just to please her ever-so-kind father. The marriage was to bring great honor to the family and Reet couldn't bring herself to disobey her father.

Reet stands there again facing her father as he asks the same question from years ago. "Are you happy with this match? You must tell me." He put his pipe down, eyes full of concern. Reet remembers wanting to tell her father that she loved another, that Jassie was a rich creep, that she had seen him with other men in very compromising positions. But she had said nothing.

Reet is startled as she hears Madhuja's voice filling the space, drowning out the in-tune birds, the off-key sister, and everything else. "Tell him the truth. Tell him you love another man. This will end differently. Tell him. Tell him the *truth*. Reet, we all create our own realties. Tell your father you don't wish to marry Jassie. Tell him now and change your future. It is up to you." Madhuja's voice is loud, strong, and chilling.

"How can I refuse my father?" Reet mumbles. She slowly begins to step away from the image. It's been years since she cried. She whimpers in pain as her chest stiffens. She falls to her knees, crying. "Bauji, Bauji," she weeps and looks up, but the scene is gone and there is just darkness.

As she weeps, the memories come flooding back, the memories of that night.

That apocalyptic night. The night that ended Reet's life as she knew it.

Reet had agreed to marry Jassie to please her beloved father.

The families had all been happy and danced around with joy. She had been angry and upset.

"Seema, you have to come with me to tell him. I have to tell him that this has happened." Reet remembers begging her sister late that night to go with her to explain to the true love of her life that she was now betrothed to another man.

Seema had been hesitant and afraid. "I don't want to go. It's so late and Bauji will be so angry if he finds out."

After a bit of convincing and some arm-twisting didn't work, Reet changed her approach. "I will never speak to you again if you don't come with me."

The emotional blackmail worked and Seema relented, stepping out into the dark, moonless night.

Now, kneeling on the cold concrete pathway, reliving that nightmare, Reet sobs even more. Then she hears Madhuja's voice.

"You have to face your demons, Reet, or those demons will kill Seema." Her words echo in the deep of the night.

"Madhuja, keep the damn money. I'm done." Reet throws the money bag and the knife on the ground, gets up and begins to run to the only open path that she can make out in the darkness.

The path narrows and then disappears.

"Seema, help me, Seema please don't leave me here." Reet hears her own voice coming from somewhere. She stops running.

"No, no, no, Madhuja, no, don't do this to me, I beg you, don't *do* this to me," Reet cries, but it's too late, the scene is the moment of horror that broke her.

Only the dim light of two street lamps illuminates everything.

Reet stares. Her mind tells her to run, but paralyzed with fear, she can't move.

It's a mostly deserted road, a back alley that the girls often used as a shortcut to their house. They are just yards away from the back door. A few moments more and they would have been home safe.

Instead, Reet sees herself on the ground being pounded by one thug as the other one chases Seema, who manages to run away.

Reet cringes. She can still smell the alcohol, and the thug's sweat. She can feel the hard, tar road under her back, the hands all over her body, those same hands ripping her pants. She can feel the pain on her face as the thug slaps her around. She can hear herself screaming, "NO, NO, NO!" She screams and screams and screams. The drunken man picks her up by her hair and slaps her. Reet hits her head on the ground. He pushes himself on top of her.

Reet watches herself about to be raped.

"I can't go through this again. Please, I am begging you, make this stop. I can't go through this again." Reet falls to her knees and begins to weep so hard her entire body shakes, hands covering tear-stained cheeks—tears she thought had long ago dried and gone to hell.

"Reet, you have to open your eyes, look at what is happening . . . look . . . *look* at what is happening."

"How can you make me see this? My sister left me to be raped."

"Reet, open your eyes. Look up. *Now.*"

Despite her fear, Reet looks up again.

The first man is so drunk he's having trouble pulling her clothes off, so he tries to put himself in her mouth. He loses balances and falls over. He picks up a stick and tries to push it into her, and the stick cuts the insides of Reet's thigh and scratches her crotch, but he can't see what he is doing in the dark. He gets frustrated and throws the stick away and punches her face.

"He assaulted you, that horrible, evil man. I am so sorry. But Seema tried her best to stop him as quickly as she could," Madhuja says.

Reet continues to stare. This can't be true. It defied a truth that every cell in her body believed: She had been abandoned by her sister to be raped by two vicious thugs.

Reet sees herself lying on the road, unconscious, and the second man is opening his pants and getting ready to try taking his turn. The light is dim. The first man is laughing and goading his friend along. "At least one of us gets to do it."

Reet simply stares. Out of the darkness, she sees little Seema coming back. She's carrying a large, half-moon-shaped knife. It's the knife Seema uses to break open coconuts, when she learns from the vendor on the street how to chop coconuts, a knife hidden from her parents.

"What the hell is going on here?" Reet says. Seema came back? With a knife?

Reet adamantly believed that Seema had deserted her, never coming back or bringing help, leaving her half-dead on the street to be raped.

What Reet sees now tells a different story. The keeper of lost memories has fulfilled her duty.

Reet watches, stunned. Seema moves quietly towards the first thug who punched Reet unconscious. He has his back turned towards the ongoing brutality and is taking a leisurely leak by the side of the road and saying, "Finish soon, and let's go get another drink before she wakes up. We can always come back. She will lie here for a while, I smacked her nice and hard."

Reet sees Seema hack the man's neck from behind. Silently, he falls. The knife, used to slashing hard coconut shells, goes through the man's neck as if through soft butter. Skin, veins, tissue, muscle; all cut with one single, powerful stroke.

The other thug is still fumbling at his clothing. "I have never had such fair skin before . . . What was that? Did you fall in the ditch peeing, moron?"

Again, a knife slashes, but it isn't Seema. The second thug is slain by Ajit, the coconut vendor. The thug's body jerks and he falls to the ground. Ajit lives in a small cardboard box on the street and he's come running, hearing the commotion.

Reet is incredulous. Her tiny sister appears to have the strength of several grown men. Reet watches as Seema leaves and returns again, this time carrying a container of kerosene. Seema slowly removes Reet's bloody shirt, and with Ajit's help drags both the bodies together, throws the shirt on top of them, pours kerosene, and then throws a lit match.

Reet watches in shock. All that time, she and her mother hated that poor coconut vendor and thought he was merely wasting Seema's time. She wants to reach out and thank Ajit. To say something. Reet feels violently ill discovering she has been taking out her rage for years on Seema for not helping her. Seema never said a word in denial.

"Seema and Ajit took you home. To avoid the shame, Seema told everyone that climbing over a stone wall, you had fallen and slipped on some embedded broken glass that cut and scratched your inner legs and crotch, and you smashed your face and head. A bad accident that could have been much worse. You were in no condition to tell the truth, and wouldn't have wanted to."

"Why didn't Seema tell me later what she did?"

"Trauma hurts our brains and our memories. Look at what it did to you. Imagine what it did to her. Maybe she did try? Do you remember? Think again."

Now, Reet recalls, Seema trying in her soft voice trying to tell her what really happened, but Reet would scream and not want to know. After trying a few times, Seema had shut down and not said anything at all.

The rain is still coming down. The gentle drops cool Reet's face. The sky lightens as the sun shows off its first morning ray. The garden is back to being filled with acres of grass and beautiful flowers. The large bushes, foreboding trees, and narrow paths are gone.

The keeper of lost memories shows Reet the way back home.

The Flower of Faith

Ajit the Coconut Vendor's story

Ajit looks at the old rickety table that holds his fortune for the day. There are three corncobs, an iron stove brimming with nearly extinguished coal embers, a lemon half-smeared with hot red pepper, and a plastic bag filled with corn silk and husks. He's sold three corncobs all evening and now there are no more customers.

Years ago, he sold coconuts, but that business died when he was accused of killing two men. He'd denied it, but the police arrested him anyway. He had no lawyer and didn't have an education. Someone in the prison told Ajit that they could only keep him if there was an eyewitness, or they found the knife supposedly used.

After a few months of questioning, the police had let Ajit go. He had lost his business, had nowhere to live, and no way of earning a living. No one wanted to know a man accused of murder. Just before Ajit decided to leave the city, Seema had come by to see him. He hadn't expected it. He'd done what he thought was the right thing, without any desire for gain. Seema had handed him a silken pouch. Before he could say anything or even see what was in the pouch, she ran away.

Inside the pouch were a few coins, some seeds, two baby-sized gold bangles, a religious picture, a small chocolate, and a note that read, "They will never find the knives. Sorry for all the trouble. I tried to tell Reet but she won't listen to me. She finds sanctuary in her denial, and strength for life in her rage. So now, my gift is that I no longer try. I did what I had to."

Ajit wanted to go back, to return all the stuff in the pouch, but something in his heart told him he needed to move on in case the family now accused him of stealing.

So Ajit had moved here, to Bombaim, so sweetly named by the long-gone Portuguese, and business had never been good.

Now Ajit winces in pain as the blisters on his feet sting. Something is festering in them and he can't figure out what it is. He digs his feet a bit deeper into the cool beach sand, hoping it will calm the burning sensation.

His table stands at the end of the beach. The view isn't only spectacular; it is free. The Sea Link bridge glitters on sunny days. On especially clear days, he can see the red dome of the Ganesh Temple across the water. Today that dome isn't visible, a thick smog everywhere. At some points, despite the smog, a gentle breeze from the Arabian Sea provides a bit of relief from the suffocating air.

Ajit looks up at the sky. On occasion when the smog breaks up, he notices the dark clouds crowding together. "Moving clouds don't rain," his mother used to tell him when he was a child. Indeed, it was only when they gathered together like a band of thugs and stayed in one place that they unleashed their wrath on the earth.

Ajit can hear the loud voice of his friend, Sudhir, at the table just a few feet away. "I will serve you in one minute. Please, please we are working as fast as we can."

Ajit looks over longingly. Sudhir has it made. He has a nice, new table with all its legs intact. Sudhir sells all kinds of corn dishes, not just corn on the cob cooked on coals. And he sells them well. Long ago, Ajit stopped wondering why. It seemed like his lot in life was to have everything taken away from him.

The sun is now drowning into the sea and the clouds are getting darker. Ajit drags his aching feet over to Sudhir's cart to see if he can help.

"Ajit, can you pass out the cups and napkins? My helper didn't come today and the line is getting really long."

Ajit moves slowly, the wounds in his foot causing shocks of pain. "I am coming to help, hold on."

He picks up the napkins and the fulfilled orders and passes them out to the people waiting, mostly patiently, in line.

A couple of hours pass and Sudhir slowly but surely starts to run out of food. "Look, the money box is filled to the top today," Sudhir whispers to Ajit as the line starts thinning.

Tiny raindrops begin to fall and the crowd starts to disperse. "Ajit, hurry up, people are leaving. Make sure they have everything," Sudhir calls as he reaches for his yellow umbrella. The umbrella is big enough to cover him and his cart and, of course, has no holes.

Sudhir says, "Okay, we're done. What a day. Made more money today than all last *week*. Ajit, clean up my area before you leave? I'll see you tomorrow. I promised Sheila, first day, first show, because her favorite hero is starring in the new movie." Sudhir pushes his cart towards the main street.

"Okay. Have a good time," Ajit says and begins to pick up the leftover corn pieces off the table, quietly popping them into his mouth.

"Why do you always help him?" a gentle voice calls out to Ajit. "At least the rain has stopped, so you aren't soaking wet out here. I know you, you're such a fool that you would clean up for him even if we were having a monsoon."

"Priest Prasad. What are you doing here?" Ajit goes to the young priest standing tall under the gulmohar trees planted on the sidewalk that lines the beach. He bends down, as a sign of respect, and touches the feet of the priest.

"No, no, don't do that. I have told you a thousand times. Only bow before God, not man." Prasad grabs Ajit's shoulders and pulls him up.

"Why in God's name do you help this idiot Sudhir? He is a user. He should have paid you for today, but no, he just uses you. You need to learn, Ajit. This is not good."

Ajit says, "I don't mind, and it's not like my cart was doing any business today. Are you walking back to the temple? Give me a minute to clean up and I will walk with you." Ajit begins to pick up all the trash.

The garbage can is overflowing and a few beggar kids are waiting patiently at Ajit's cart, as they do every night.

"See, now you will give them your leftover food. My friend, what will you eat for dinner? Pray tell me?" Prasad says.

Ajit picks up the few leftovers from his cart and hands them to the beggar boys who jump with glee and thank him profusely. He then looks at Prasad. "Of all the people in this world, you, a man of God, should not be asking me that. It is, Priest Prasad, as my mother used to say, Jako rahke Saiyan, mar sake Na Koi. He is my savior and I believe He will protect me and provide me with a meal tonight."

The beachfront has almost cleared out due to the rain, and the billboards—now all digital—are boldly advertising the next best place to get people to spend their money singing, drinking, and gambling.

Priest Prasad and Ajit stop and look at a live TV screen that has recently been installed near the beach. A rich young movie star worked with a local cable company to stream every mundane moment of his life, and there were throngs of people constantly watching, wishing, hoping that somehow their lives would be turned around from the chawl to the bungalow.

Today the screen isn't showing the reality show, but breaking news of what has been thought to be an urban legend: a futuristic death machine known as the Nirvana Train that was found under the grounds of an old step-well in Shahajahanabad. The picture of a young woman flashes across the screen with a plea from a man in a hospital bed, "My wife, Sehar, is missing. If you have seen her, please tell her to come home. Sehar, if you're watching, I want you to come home." The man, Rishi, is crying. The reporter begins to talk again, informing the viewing public that the train failed this dying man and that his wife disappeared under suspicious circumstances.

"The Nirvana Train has provided this man with no nirvana, only nightmares," the dramatic reporter signs off with an arrogant smirk.. The reality show returns.

"I wonder if that train really offers a painless death?" Ajit says. "If I could get on that, I would. You know—unlike my life—at least my death would be pain-free."

Prasad places a hand on his friend's shoulder, unsure of what to say. Life in this metropolis is becoming harder by the minute for those who aren't blessed by Lakshmi, the Goddess of wealth and prosperity.

The men quietly make their way to the temple, about a kilometer or so from the beach.

Other than the loud and gaudy digital billboards, there isn't any activity on the roads. At dusk they're usually filled with tired commuters heading home, but today are eerily quiet with only the occasional car whizzing by.

"There is an automobile boycott today. Some politician must have complained about pollution," Prasad says, helping Ajit push the cart.

"Do these people even realize how good they have it? I sometimes wonder. They have a car, but they choose not to use it." Ajit stops to check his festering, painful foot.

They arrive at the temple just as the assistant priest is closing the doors to the main entrance. The sweet scent of jasmine incense is a welcoming relief from the stale smells of the city.

"Oh wait, let me bring my cart in, please," Ajit pleads and the young priest steps aside. "The strike seems to have affected the temple as well. Where is everyone?" Ajit notices there are no lines in front of the temple gate, as is customary this time of the evening, and the gates are closing earlier than usual.

"We were told to shut down as there is a threat of rioting this evening. Come inside, you will be safe here." The young priest gets everyone inside and shuts the gates.

Inside, it's God's own country with a strikingly green garden laden with blooming roses, water fountains bubbling with clean, clear water, and the temple in the center of the garden that holds statues of several gods and enough good vibes to heal any broken spirit. Ajit adores the temple and its inhabitants.

There are six rooms in a cluster. The priests, the cleaners, and the temple cook live there. When Ajit had first arrived, he slept under the stars. But a few months later, at the urging of Prasad, the people had agreed to share one of the tiny rooms, a space barely enough to hold a grown man and a mattress for the ever-smiling Ajit. In return, Ajit helped around the temple, cleaning, planting, singing, and generally spreading goodwill.

"So did you make any money today? Or do I have to feed you again?" the temple cook, Chinmay, calls out to Ajit.

Before Ajit can say anything, Prasad says, "What do you think? Our man here is helping that idiot again and then—yes, you guessed it—fed the kids all the food from his own cart."

Chinmay, a round man with a well-oiled bald head, laughs heartily.

"You are lucky I like you, Ajit. Now come here and eat some dinner before the rains come back and the lights go out again."

Ajit parks the broken cart in front of his room. He goes inside and brings out a small stainless-steel plate and heads to the temple kitchen. It's a kitchen in name only: a makeshift kerosene stove sitting on a concrete platform. Chinmay sits beside it scooping out the rice and lentil mixture that is dinner for everyone. The temple lost favor with some of its wealthier patrons after it started sheltering victims of a gay-bashing movement. The loss of income meant no kitchen and very meager scraps to eat, but the people stayed in faith and happily shared whatever they had with Ajit.

A young priest sits down beside Prasad and Ajit to eat. "Priest Prasad, that tooth doctor, Dr. Meera, came in and set up camp today just before morning prayers. I really like her, but there is this one issue."

"What issue?"

"She always makes me show her my teeth. What kind of woman is that? Asking a man to constantly open his mouth? Preposterous! She said she's coming again next week. Oh, and today she cleaned the teeth of about twenty beggar kids. What good does that do? You tell me. What is the point of cleaning the teeth of these filthy urchins? We had quite a drama-filled afternoon." As the priest talks, the others giggle.

Chinmay says, "She is really a good lady, but I would be happy if she never asks me to open my mouth again. Anyway, eat up before the night sky begins to terrorize us again. Last night, there was hail."

The group eats in grateful silence.

"How was your day, Priest Prasad? You were in Shahajahanabad this morning?" Chinmay is known to be nosy and cannot help himself.

"Yes, I have a friend there, Angela. We grew up together." Between bites, Prasad haltingly explains that the situation in Shahajahanabad was the worst thing he had ever seen. Two young people, whom Sister Angela cared about deeply, had apparently committed suicide. Their next of kin wasn't responding or available—Prasad isn't sure of that, but says that the local police were unwilling to allow Angela take the bodies.

Prasad's brother, who was with the Shahajahanabad police,

had said, "I will register them as suicides because you are asking, Prasad, and since you are a man of God. But something seems off here." Regardless, there was no evidence of foul play so he was able to get the bodies released for Angela to arrange their last rites.

Angela wanted Prasad to perform the last rites and honor the deceased. Angela dressed Damini as a bride—at least in death, she could die a bride. As the bodies burned, side by side on a sandalwood pyre, an odd scent had filled the air.

"What in the world is that smell?" she'd asked Prasad. "I think that smells like frangipani, but I don't see that flower anywhere here."

Angela had been inconsolable and Prasad felt in his heart that he would be returning several times to give support. At his insistence, and for a sense of closure, he persuaded Angela to distribute their ashes around the rose bushes outside the hospital.

Prasad tells them, "I can imagine why the man with terminal cancer killed himself, even before their wedding, but I cannot even begin to understand why the woman did, if they were about to be wed. And she was a pain healer." He stops eating. "You know, both committed suicide on the same night, but in *different* places. What went wrong? If it had been a suicide pact, why not die together?"

Chinmay now wishes he hadn't asked. All Prasad ever seems to do these days is cremations with macabre stories behind them. Why could he just not have gone to Shahajahanabad to, say, attend a wedding?

They eat quietly as the rain returns. It's gentle, but the fire under the stove is out. Usually the young girl who sweeps the temple floors clears the makeshift kitchen, but she doesn't appear to be around.

Chinmay begins to clear the area, muttering something about God needing to be kinder to his motley crew at the temple. Ajit picks up everyone's plates and takes them to the community sink to wash them. Prasad retreats to the main temple to prepare for the early morning prayer.

Chinmay disappears into his room along with everything from the kitchen except the still-hot stove.

Ajit slowly walks to his tiny room. He stops at the entrance when he notices that one of his very few possessions in this world, a tiny terra cotta pot, is broken. He bends to pick up the mess and sees a miniscule, shriveled-up plant lying among the pieces.

Wow, the seeds actually sprouted, he says to himself. The pot brings back painful memories. The tiny plant had sprouted from the seeds that little Seema gave him when he was released from jail.

The seeds were in a handkerchief sachet. At first Ajit had just held on to them. When he finally moved into the temple, he decided to plant them. The temple priest had given him the pot. No matter what he did—added soil, water, and even crushed rose leaves at the advice of Chinmay—the seeds didn't sprout. A young priest had even said a prayer over the seeds, but nothing had happened. Ajit had just about given up.

Now, looking at the pot, he smiles at the little sprout.

Somewhere deep in his heart, Ajit can't help but think the sprout is a good sign and that something positive has finally happened for Seema. He has often wondered about her.

He had guarded the seeds with his life—their monetary value

was probably nothing, but the way in which she'd handed them to him had always made Ajit feel there was a message hidden in them.

He looks up at the sky and mumbles a prayer of thanks. "I know this is your way of showing me that Seema, and whatever ails her, is all fine now," he says and smiles.

The raindrops begin to strike the compound with a harshness Ajit hasn't seen before.

He picks up the small sprout, takes it into the room, and closes the paper-thin door behind him.

Ajit had told Chinmay, when he first put the thin doors up for all the temple rooms, "The doors are nothing more than an old thin sheet of wood and will break down soon, I know, but at least during these crazy rains, it keeps the water out."

His room, despite being a sliver larger than a dog house, had distinct advantages, like electricity for instance. A rich temple patron had an electrician install wiring, light bulbs, and fans in the musty, dingy rooms. The generous man also paid the electric bill every month. This was before the temple provided shelter for the gay community. Now, each day of electricity was a bonus as the temple staff expected the patron would back out any day now.

The tiny light bulb gives Ajit's room a gentle glow.

"What on earth is that smell?" Ajit says out loud and then realizes it's coming from the plant in his hand. It is an odd-looking plant. The shriveled leaves are tiny, but there are wool-like structures attached to the end of the thin branches. Ajit plucks one serrated leaf and smells it. The citrus smell reminds him of the orange trees in his village. He smells the leaf again;

119

this time lemon is more pronounced. Maybe Seema gave him lemon tree seeds.

Habitually, Ajit bites into the leaf and his eyes widen in wonder.

The leaf tastes sweet, like jaggery. Ajit has only tasted jaggery two or three times, all of them at this temple during festivities. He knows the taste. He often craved it so much that he offered to clean the altar which usually had remnants of offerings of jaggery, and he picked up the little crumbs and savored them.

"Jaggery is not made for the poor," he always tells Chinmay.

Ajit looks again at the leaf and decides to take another bite. Again—the smell and taste contradict each other.

Ajit gently places the plant into his other worldly possession: a glass tumbler.

"You can have my tea tumbler for the night, little lemon-honey plant, but what will I use for tea tomorrow?" He pours some water into the tumbler from a bottle that Chinmay has given him. He places it under the only decoration in the room: a photograph of his mother as a young woman.

He looks at the weathered old picture: a black and white photo of a woman with tight braids, wearing a dark saree and sitting on a park bench. She's holding an infant in her lap and gazing down at him with gentle eyes. Her tiny wrists are covered with bangles and she wears a thick gold necklace. She was, he was told, a wealthy princess.

"Ah, but how luck changes in an instant." Ajit smiles at the photo, a constant reminder that you become what you believe. His mother, born into prostitution, believed she was destined to be a princess and *was* married into a royal family. Her untimely death, shortly after his sixth birthday, changed the direction of his life. His father's family didn't want to accept that Ajit, a baby born of a wedding to a prostitute, could be their heir, so they dropped him off at a temple after bribing a priest. He only had this picture, which was in his pocket at the time. The priest worried they may come back to kill Ajit, since the family was very wealthy and the matriarch had expressed worries about Ajit growing up and eventually asking for his share of their money. The little boy was so sweet and kind that the priest took pity on him and sent Ajit to a temple in the mountains to make sure the family couldn't hurt him in any way.

Ajit had moved from city to city since then, sometimes helping out at temples, tending gardens, selling coconuts and corn from a tiny cart and, of course, trying to find the meaning of his inconsequential existence. Ajit's only memory of his mother or her story was what the temple priest had told him before he left the mountains, and whatever his failing memory remembered from the old photo.

He touches the photo and says, "It is a lonely life."

The storm outside rages. The rain is pounding hard on the roof of the tiny room. A few drops leak through.

Ajit quickly puts a plastic bag over the photo, hoping the rain won't be able to destroy his only connection to his childhood.

He then turns his attention to his bed, a bamboo mat and pillow courtesy of Priest Prasad. He sits down on the bamboo mat and folds his hands in prayer, as he does each night, and begins his chant of the night, the Gayatri Mantra. It was one of the few things he does remember fondly from his childhood. His mother insisted that each night, before bed, he finish the Gayatri

Mantra ten times and then express gratitude for what God had given him. She had told him that the night he reached a hundred new things to be grateful for would be the night the Universe would grant Ajit anything his heart desired.

Ajit was ashamed that he couldn't count to one hundred. He only knew his numbers to thirty.

He begins his gratefulness chant with thanks for Priest Prasad, the seed that sprouted, the success of his friend Sudhir, the kindness of Chinmay, not being around when the tooth doctor came, the pouring rain that shut out all other sounds and soothed him to sleep, and his aching feet, which still carried him wherever he wanted to go.

"Oh, wait—" He looks at his feet. His aching, wounded, infected, dirty feet no longer hurt. He moves his toes. Nothing. No pain. He stands up and walks around. Still no pain. This makes no sense. No wounds, no festering flesh, and no pain.

"It's happening. I'm finally losing my mind. This isn't real. This is not happening. I want you to stop all this," he says out loud to no one, and then sits down again.

Ajit pinches his foot in a few places. Again, no pain.

He begins walking around again. The cold cement floor under his feet is soothing.

"What's going on?" He begins to run in place, putting pressure on his heel and toes.

Ajit hurries outside and knocks on the next door. A very sleepy Chinmay opens it.

"What is the matter? Is the temple on fire?"

"My foot. My foot. Look! Did you add some medicine or magical potion in tonight's dinner and not tell me?" Ajit is shouting so he can be heard above the downpour. The rain hits the back of his shirt, his pants, his feet, but he stands, oblivious to it all.

"Go to bed, Ajit. You're going crazy. Stop selling in the heat. It's affecting your brain. If I *had* a magical potion, you think I would waste it on you?" The cook slams his door, which falls off the hinges.

Ajit doesn't give up and knocks on the next door. The young priest knows nothing.

Ajit moves on to Prasad's door.

"What is it, Ajit? You look like you've seen a ghost," Prasad says. Ajit explains again.

The priest takes a deep breath and then asks, "Can I take a look in your room?"

The men go to Ajit's room and immediately the lemony smell hits Prasad.

"That smell, where is that coming from?" Prasad asks in an excited but hushed tone.

Ajit points to the plant.

Prasad touches the plant to be sure it is what he thinks it is.

Small hailstones pound the fragile tin roof creating a loud, scary thudding noise. *The Gods are pelting the earth because of us ungrateful humans*, Ajit thinks, but doesn't say anything. He kicks the wall and it makes him cry in pain.

"What are you doing, Ajit?" Prasad says. "Stop that. Your pain is gone and I know why."

"Why? What did Chinmay give me? That's the only meal I had today."

"Ajit, it isn't the food. It's this plant. This is a gift from the

123

Lord himself. This is a great healing plant. I have read about it in scriptures, but have never seen it in real life." Prasad closes his eyes, joins his hands together, and bows down in front of the plant as Ajit stares on, still confused.

"How did you get this?" the priest asks Ajit, who relays the story about saving Seema.

Prasad nods as he listens. "That child has blessed you with a very rare gift. Share the gift of healing that this plant provides, but don't tell anyone about it. This blessing can quickly become a curse."

"But how can I use it?"

"The answer is already in you. Go sleep and ask the Divine for guidance."

Prasad wishes Ajit a good night and heads to bed, but sleep is lost on Ajit.

Finally, exhaustion catches up with him and he falls asleep with a smile on his face.

The next morning, Ajit first checks to make sure the plant is still there. It appears to have grown a little, the leaves are larger and brighter, and there are two buds at the end of one of the branches. As he stares at it, an idea hits him.

He rushes out to the tap, washes his face and rinses his mouth. Even as he's rinsing, he begins to sing praises of the good Lord, and the good Goddess in the form of Seema, who gave him such a gift.

As he's getting ready to leave, he notices the tooth doctor, Dr. Meera, entering the temple and tries to avoid her.

"Ajit, you can run from me, but you will come back here and I *will* be sure to fix your teeth," she says sweetly. He smiles awkwardly and runs to the nearby vegetable market where the fat man usually gives him the corn to sell on his cart.

"No, no, I'm not giving you anything more. You give everything away for free and I get no money from you." The fat man is mad and uncooperative.

"Please, one last chance? I need some onions, tomatoes, and lemons as well. I promise to pay you back by the end of day today. If not, no more? Please? I just want to try one more time." Ajit smiles and begs, but knows his chances are very slim.

The fat man, who only wears pajamas but no shirts, eyes him as he moves his hand over his round belly and picks tiny little things out of his exposed navel.

"One more chance. If I don't get my money this evening, I will come to that temple and beat you with my shoe," the man says. Then he calls to his skinny assistant to give Ajit what he wants.

Ajit takes the bag of vegetables, profusely thanks the fat man, and makes a dash back to the temple. In his room, he peels and dices all the vegetables, seasons them with lemon juice, and adds slivers of the magical leaf to the mix. He places the mixture in the only large bowl the temple owns (vowing to apologize to Chinmay for stealing it for the day), places the bowl on his broken-down cart, and heads to the beach.

Sudhir is already there, selling his corn to an ever-growing crowd.

"You are taking a holiday or what? Where have you been? I need help," Sudhir yells at Ajit.

"Let me just sell my snack and I will be there," Ajit replies as he pushes his cart over the sandy shore to his favorite position.

"No one eats your stuff. Throw it away and come here," Sudhir says.

"But—" Ajit parks his cart and goes to help his friend. The sun beats down on them and their customers, but the corn sells, and sells fast. Sudhir sells out.

"Now I'll go home to Sheila. See you tomorrow." Sudhir pushes his empty cart and pats his full pocket as he leaves the beach and a forlorn Ajit behind.

Ajit returns to his own cart and begins to call out to people, "Fresh, spicy vegetable snacks, please come and try."

No one ventures close. Despite his best efforts to continue to be magnanimous, his heart fills with anger and his eyes with rage. He hates Sudhir.

If only he had focused on his own cart. Now the fat man will be mad, Chinmay will be angry too and, of course, there is no money.

Ajit wipes his tears and begins packing his cart to leave when a young man approaches. "One plate, please."

Ajit hands him the sweet-savory mound of food. The stranger takes the plate, pays, and leaves.

"At least someone came," Ajit says as he looks around for the beggar kids. Perhaps he can feed them tonight, if nothing else.

Just as he's about to call the young beggar boys, the young man returns. "My mother is in the car over there and she really loved your dish. Can we have three more?"

Ajit begins preparing the plate, and the young man talks on the phone. "Yes, Ma, I'm getting some more. I don't think this dish cured your headache, I think you were hungry and eating something helped. Yes, I'm getting it. Hold on—"

Slowly a line begins to form and in about twenty minutes the magical mix sells out. Ajit pushes his cart back to the temple and stops to pay the fat man, who is stunned that he's actually getting money from this village idiot.

The next three days, Ajit runs out of food, each day quicker than the previous one. On the tenth day, his dish sells out in under an hour. Ajit rushes home to tell Prasad the good news, but instead is greeted by Sudhir standing at the temple entrance.

"My friend, what are you doing here? Oh, I have to tell you something—" Ajit starts to say, but Sudhir steps forward and slaps Ajit hard across the face.

"You bastard, you are taking my business away. After all I have done to help you? How are you doing this? What are you feeding these people? You can't even cook."

Ajit stands there stunned.

"What are you talking about, my friend? Your business is going great. I'm just selling a few plates of food. I haven't sold anything in such a long time. I thought you would be happy for me."

Suddenly, two men come from behind and grab Ajit by the collar.

"Bring him into his room," says Sudhir. The men drag a struggling Ajit into his room. The space is so tight they can barely stand in there together.

"Now, you will talk," says Sudhir as he shuts the door. He produces a knife from a bag.

"Talk? What do you want to know? I don't understand—" Ajit can't complete the sentence because Sudhir plunges the knife into his thigh as one of the men holds his mouth shut.

"I am giving you one last chance to tell me. What are you

127

adding to the food? Is it hashish? Ganja? What are you adding? Why are people lining up? It is *not* for your vegetables and certainly *not* for your cooking." Sudhir's voice booms.

Ajit points to the plant. The wound in his leg is bleeding profusely, spreading red all over the floor. The thugs still have their hands over his mouth.

"This? What, you think I am an idiot? *This*?" Sudhir bends down, plucks a leaf from the plant and puts it in his mouth. He spits it out in a second.

"This tastes like turd. You're lying to me. I will *not* forgive you for this." Sudhir plunges the knife into Ajit's abdomen.

Prasad's voice is heard from outside. "What is going on in there? Ajit? Open this door!"

Sudhir and his thugs open the door and he tells Prasad, "We're leaving. If you open your mouth, you will be next. And tell this bastard, if he lives, that he can never be seen again at the beach."

Prasad rushes in to help Ajit. He bends down and takes his hand. Ajit's eyes are rolling in the back of his head, and foam is coming out of his mouth.

"He needs medical help," Chinmay is now at the door. "I am going to call a doctor."

Prasad gets up, tells Chinmay to wait for a few minutes, and closes the door. He plucks a few leaves of the plant, crushes them in his hands, and applies them to Ajit's wounds. Slowly, the skin begins to heal and the bleeding stops. The wound in the abdomen is deep and Prasad worries the healing plant may not be enough, but then he stops, closes his eyes, and exhales. "I must keep the faith."

In an hour or so, just as the dark sky begins to provide a soothing blanket to the suffering earth, Ajit opens his eyes and stares at Prasad. "I did not betray him. I did not lie to him," Ajit whispers.

There is furious knocking on the door. Both men stiffen. "It must be him again, he wants to finish me off," Ajit says. "He will break that door. It isn't strong."

Before Prasad can answer, they hear Chinmay. "Priest Prasad, open the door. Please. I have to tell you something."

Prasad opens the door and Chinmay doesn't say a word but points towards the temple entrance.

Sudhir is standing there, his face covered with ghastly lesions, pus, and blood oozing from pimples, his hands red with bruises and scars.

Ajit drags himself to the door and nearly cries out when he sees Sudhir under the light of a street lamp.

"I can help him. I know the plant can cure him," he says. Prasad holds him back.

"The plant will not work on him. It works on those with clean hearts. His heart is polluted. The plant just brings out what is inside you. I'm glad you're better. Now get ready to face your *real* fear: the tooth doctor, Dr. Meera, is coming for you all tomorrow."

The Weeping Sky

Dr. Meera's story

The smell of cow dung mixed with roses and sandalwood incense assails Dr. Meera's nostrils as she enters the temple.

A young girl, Geeta, tinier than a rose bush, is busy sweeping the entrance with a broom made of sirki grass. The broom makes a swooshing sound as she gracefully moves it from side to side.

"The priest keeps the broom inside, under his cot, so that it doesn't get damaged in the rain. But I sleep outside, under the sky," Geeta had told Meera a couple of years ago. At the time, Meera had tried to help her, but the cranky resident priest thought Geeta was nothing more than a nuisance.

Finally, when the cranky priest passed on at the grand old age of a hundred and four, a startlingly handsome new priest had come in. Prasad had built a small hut for Geeta, and Meera ensured the hut had a mattress, sanitary supplies, a case filled with beauty products (Geeta did not even know what a perfume was before she met Meera) and a few travel magazines. Geeta couldn't read but gazed fondly at pictures of the snowy Alps, rain-soaked streets of London, the glorious cherry blooms of Tokyo, and her most favorite: the endless romantic pictures of Paris. She ripped out pictures she liked and created a makeshift ceiling cover using the photographs. At night, a weak bulb in the hut would light up and she would stare at the beautiful pictures.

"I dream in color now," she told Meera.

Geeta's hut leaks like crazy during the rainy season, which destroys the ceiling cover she creates so lovingly. Meera once suggested she could buy Geeta a tarp, or even pay for a permanent roof.

"Actually, Dr. Meera, I love it when it rains. When it rains, you see, my mother weeps for me," Geeta said, with her tiny hand over her heart, and no tarp was ever put up.

Meera fondly watches Geeta meticulously sweep the temple floor.

Today, Meera hasn't come to the temple for cleaning anyone's teeth, or for Geeta. She's here for something Meera never imagined could happen—she's here to get married.

There is no wedding party though. No mom or dad, and no friends.

Just her and the love of her life, Atul, who should be arriving soon.

Meera couldn't convince her family to agree. Atul said there was no point telling *his* family. So his suggestion was they have a temple wedding and then fly to Singapore for their honeymoon. Meera smiles. *This is going to be a great day.*

"Dr. Meera, Dr. Meera, look what I made for you." Geeta leaves her broom and runs across the green-tiled courtyard to the banyan tree. She reaches down towards the base of the tree and pulls out two marigold and rose garlands from a plastic bag. She holds them in her arms and rushes back to Meera.

"Here, here, I got the flowers from the garden in the back.

Don't tell Chinmay. He will be mad. Just tell him you bought this, and here, here is a scarf for you from the Temple of Peace. I had a little money that I had saved up. Every new bride needs the red scarf of protection."

Meera wants to ask why Geeta thinks, first that she needs to be protected and second, how a scarf will protect her. But she doesn't want to hurt the young girl's feelings.

Meera is an atheist all the way, yet here today she can't help but wonder why God, if he exists, put this beautiful, big-hearted child in such appalling circumstances. She hugs and thanks Geeta, and then checks her watch. It's almost time. She is here, in a place she doesn't hold sacred, because Atul seems to think they need the blessings of the good Lord.

Meera had, of course, tried to dissuade him from this whole temple wedding thing. "Atul, just look at all the honor killings, the genocides. All in the name of religion."

He shook his head. "I disagree. That is just a few bad eggs."

"Fine, but then what about . . . illnesses, poverty, rapes, murders, abductions—what kind of God allows that? No, no thanks. No God for me," she had insisted, but then lost out to his insistence.

"If you love me, you will say yes to this plan."

So here she is for the man she loves, hoping this circus will end soon so they can go to the courthouse, sign their wedding papers, have a glass of bubbly, and then head to the airport.

Meera feels Geeta tugging at her saree.

"Dr. Meera, you look nice in this. No more pant shirt today?" Her smile makes Meera happy as a human, but cringe as a dentist. All those rotting teeth.

Geeta refuses to have her teeth fixed. Meera has invited her umpteen times to the teeth-cleaning and cavity-fixing camp she runs for street kids, but she never comes. "One of these days, I am going to clean and fix your teeth, young lady," Meera says in her most stern voice, but Geeta just laughs.

"You are even wearing jewelry. Now, wear my scarf, please? It will take care of you. I also think it will make you look extra beautiful."

Meera smiles and places the scarf around her neck. Geeta claps with glee and then pulls Meera's arm, leading her into the inner sanctum of the temple. Meera sneaks a quick peak at her phone, but there is no news from Atul. *Probably just looking for his favorite shirt.*

"Dr. Meera! So nice to see you. No henna on your hands for the wedding? We must fix that." Prasad smiles at the kind woman. He turns around and begins to look for premade henna tubes that Geeta often leaves lying around. He finds one and offers it to her.

Dressed in a simple red saree, a few bangles, and a slim gold chain, Meera is the least bridal of any brides he has ever seen in this part of town. Most brides these days, he often tells the other priests, come in wearing enough gold to pass off as an advertisement for a jewelry store, but they have no real sparkle in their spirit. Only their gold glitters.

"Try this henna, you'll love it. We're so happy you are getting married here. You have helped so many of us. This is something small for you." Prasad gives her a bag. She opens it and finds a statue of the Goddess Lakshmi.

"She will guide you and bring you prosperity in your new

life," he says. Meera nods and graciously accepts.

"Thank you, Priest Prasad. You are so kind, but no time for henna now. Atul will be here soon. Do you have what you need for the ceremony?"

"Yes, yes—see, we have coconut, milk, sugar, fresh flowers, incense—and I see you brought garlands. Now all we need is the groom." Prasad smiles brightly and begins to arrange all the items. Meera's driver had come by last night and delivered everything. Atul had told Meera to look up the wedding samagri list on the internet when she asked what was needed.

"Thank you, Priest Prasad. I'm glad you're back in time to conduct this. How was your trip to Shahajahanabad? I understand it was under some unpleasant circumstance?"

Prasad nods and then explains the double suicide of a young healer named Damini and the love of her life, Amrit.

"This morning I have been trying to help my friend, Sister Angela, contact Damini's sister, Yamini. Angela is very disturbed that there was no family at the cremation. For either of the two. We still cannot find the sister. We can locate a single camel in a desert, but even in this great age of satellites, you can't find someone if they don't wish to be found."

Meera wants to interrupt and ask him again about what kind of a compassionate God would allow this, but thinks better of it.

"I'll wait outside for him. Is that okay?" she asks. He nods and continues to arrange the items for the wedding.

Meera places the gifted Goddess in her purse and heads outside the main sanctum and sits down on an intricate, carved wooden bench. While she has visited the temple for several years now as a dentist, today everything feels different. She notices things unseen before. The flowers etched on the bench—she recognizes them all—marigolds, lotus, sunflowers. She smiles at how they all intertwine with one another naturally, seamlessly, effortlessly. The red doors of the temple, the pale green walls, the tree in the center with pieces of red cloth tied around all the branches. Each piece holding the wish of someone who wants to pray for something and hopes the knotted cloth will magically solve their problem.

She looks up from the bench and notices Geeta has gone back to sweeping the entrance. She catches Geeta looking at her rather sadly. She chalks it up to the fact that the child thinks this marriage means that the doctor won't be available as much. She smiles warmly at Geeta. Meera often talks about Geeta with Atul and wonders why she stays here, what keeps her here, and if she will ever leave. Atul never shows the least bit of interest.

"You're a doctor. You should be spending time with the elite ladies of the city. Why the hell do you waste time on a maid? A sweeper at that."

The thought of Atul again tugs at her heart. *Where the hell is he?*

***

Meera never thought she would be married, much less to a man like Atul, the heir to a diamond empire. Her purpose in life had always been service to others. As a child, she would make sandwiches with leftover bread and white butter, and distribute it to the beggar children who lived in the slum behind her house. As a teenager, she would often spend time at the local school for the blind, reading stories to them, but mostly just listening to them and being a friend.

As an adult and a dentist, her practice was flourishing. She used the money from the rich patients to host free dental camps at temples around the country. Many times, other physicians would join her and they would also vaccinate people, pass out contraception and sanitary napkins.

While Meera was perfectly happy fixing people's smiles, her parents were thoroughly unhappy about it all. All this doctor stuff was great, but Meera wasn't married and, according to her mother, she was dangerously close to the spinster age—twenty-eight. Both parents were so worried about finding their daughter the perfect husband that they placed matrimonial ads in newspapers, websites, local newsletters, and showed her photo upon photo of aging, paunchy, balding men who would make perfect providers.

"I *have* money. I don't need a man to provide for me. If I marry, *if* being the operative word here, I want to marry for love," Meera would protest.

"Love? All this is New Age rubbish. I've been married to your father for thirty-seven years and we didn't have this love rubbish. What is this love business? You watch too many movies. All this only happens on screen. In real life, it's about creating a stable life and a home to raise children in." Her mother was relentless.

There is no one more determined than an Indian mother who wants to find the right match for her daughter, Meera learned. Her mother upped the ante and called astrologers, matchmakers, mothers of eligible boys, and even a newly widowed doctor or two asking them to come see Meera. Meera refused all the suitors, much to her mother's chagrin.

"You are getting so old, Meera. Stop all this work nonsense

or you will only get widowed men or fat, balding bachelors to marry you." It was her mother's last resort before breaking down into inconsolable tears each time Meera said no.

Meera once told her friends that she often wondered if the story her mother told was to justify to herself why she didn't marry a man she loved. Her parents lived together like happy roommates. They discussed the color of the curtains, the chicken in the curry, the sweetness of the figs, the choking pollution of the city, the affairs that their maid had with various street vendors, the failings of their daughter, the budget of the new government . . . but she has never seen them hold hands, kiss, hug, or touch each other in any way, so much so that Meera often joked that she had to be a child of immaculate conception.

When she finally found Atul, she thought her parents would be thrilled. But, of course, they weren't.

"He's not our type," her mother said.

What exactly is our type?, Meera wanted to ask, but she was no glutton for punishment and let it go.

***

Meera begins to fiddle with her hair as she waits patiently for the love of her life to arrive. She smiles as she recalls that, going against tradition, she was the one who had proposed. She had arranged a beautiful dinner on a yacht on a private pond at a country club. After caviar, oysters, and Champagne, she proposed to him, on one knee and all. At first, he had been shocked, but then he accepted the thrifty ring, they made love in the boat, and Atul said he was looking forward to the wedding.

Meera wonders if she should have put her hair in a fancy bun for the ceremony. Right now it flows down her back.

Atul loves her hair and often runs his fingers through it, something she has never seen her father do with her mother. Her mother's hair is even thicker and longer, but is treated like her life—tightly bound.

The skies darken. The monsoons have long gone, but clearly someone forgot to inform the September sky.

"The dark clouds are pulling together for a cleansing experience," Geeta says from across the temple courtyard.

Prasad pokes his head out of the main chamber to ask, "Dr. Meera, the auspicious hour is here. Is Atul stuck in traffic? I heard it's pretty messy out there. Some protests are going on around the city."

"Good question. Let me call him again," Meera says.

She dials Atul's number just as the thunder sounds and startles her, and she drops her phone.

The thunder is jarring, sharp and loud. Meera looks at the sky, a little confused.

The noise gets louder. *It's like someone has taken a sharp knife and is slicing the heart of the clouds and they are screaming in pain.*

Prasad comes running out of the temple.

Geeta drops the broom and hurries to Meera.

"Oh, don't worry. Just some nasty lightning. It should pass soon," Meera murmurs to Geeta.

But the look on Geeta's face isn't fear.

Geeta stands there, staring at Meera and then at Prasad. Her eyes are wide open and she is struggling to get the words out. "Dr. Meera, there is . . . there is something, you have to see."

Meera attributes the child's mumbling to the fear of the dreadful impending weather.

She redials Atul on her phone, which she's grateful didn't break when it fell.

No response.

Meera says to Geeta, trying to break the tension, "What is the point of having a phone but not answering it? I think he's just fashionably late. He is the princess in our relationship—he takes forever to pick out his clothes, hours to shower and get dressed, and never, ever makes it anywhere on time." She stops short of adding that Atul comes from a family that has more money than God (any God) and all of life's etiquettes and practicalities are wasted on him.

Meera had told him once, "You know, Atul, with all your vices—your fancy cars, your drinking the best scotch, your five-star dinners—I find it very amusing that you believe in God." He laughed and said he believed in God because he wanted to make sure that when his time came, he had a power bigger than he was to ask forgiveness for his scarlet sins.

Meera and Atul fell in love when Atul came to see her about a painful broken tooth. It was love at first sight, and now they'd been dating for a year. His father was a famous politician—or infamous, as the case may be—and that's why her parents were against this wedding. Atul's money came from his mother's side, diamond merchants. Meera had never met his mother but was sure a working-class dentist wasn't their idea of the ideal daughter-in-law.

"Dr. Meera, where is he?" Prasad asks again. "The auspicious moment will pass soon." He then returns and heads back into the temple to complete preparations. The thunder, at least for the moment, has settled down.

"I'm calling him. I'll let you know. I'm sure he will be here soon. Some men just don't answer their phones." Meera is also annoyed. *Why must he be late to his own wedding at a venue his own choosing?*

Meera's phone rings. She looks hopefully at the screen. It isn't Atul—it's her mother. She ignores the call.

Geeta, who has been standing by her side all this time, calls out in a shrill voice, "Dr. Meera, please look up from your phone. Look in front of you."

Meera looks up and is stunned. Not caring that she is cussing in front of the priest, Meera says, "What is this nonsense? Who the hell is doing this? Priest Prasad, come out this minute, what the hell is going on here?"

Prasad rushes out to see what Meera is so upset about and he stops, shocked. "What in God's name?"

It's raining harder than they have ever seen before.

The raindrops, the size of pearls, are hitting the green tiles of the compound. They are incessant, reminiscent of the monsoon rains. Except with one big difference—the rain drops are red. Deep red rain is pelting the courtyard.

Meera is frightened even more when she sees Prasad trembling.

"We have polluted the earth so much that nature is punishing us," Meera says, trying to make sense of the horror.

The two simply stand as the raindrops batter the ground.

Geeta says, pointing to a puddle of red water that has formed in the main courtyard, right in front of the inner sanctum, "Dr. Meera, there is something you need to see. Look carefully. My mother speaks to you."

"What are you talking about? Your mother? I don't understand—"

Instead of answering, Geeta continues to point. Something tugs at Meera's heart. Geeta grabs Meera and pulls her away from the shelter of the building and into the rain.

"Have you lost your mind, Geeta? What are you doing? I will get wet. I don't want to get wet. I'm getting married."

Geeta pulls harder and harder. She is fiercely strong for such a young child.

The rain seeps into Meera's clothes, her hair is drenched, the rain splashes her face in such a way that she appears to be crying red tears. The scarf around her neck expands and covers her shoulders, chest, and hands. Almost like it's shielding her from the rain. Geeta's words echo in her head. *The scarf will protect you.*

Prasad follows them out into the rain.

"Geeta, I really care for you, but this is ridiculous. How could you pull me out into this mess? Who knows what chemicals we've used to destroy our lakes and ponds, and now all those chemicals are raining down on us."

Prasad says, "Yes, child. Let her go. We can all go back in and then you can tell her what you want." His hands are shaking and he tries to steady himself.

Geeta looks fondly at Meera, the doctor who has done so much for everyone, the selfless savior from bad, rotting teeth, the kind angel of homeless adults, the only one who tries to bribe little children with bananas instead of sweets if they get their teeth cleaned. The compassionate—and soon unfortunate—doctor. Geeta gestures to a puddle.

Meera peers down. She sees Atul reflected in the water and turns to Geeta. "What kind of black magic is this? I care for you like my own and this is what you're doing? You're ruining my special day with some black magic trick?"

"My mother is speaking to you. Listen with your heart."

Meera looks again.

The image becomes clearer. Atul and a beautiful, well-dressed woman are sitting together in an airplane. First class, no less. The woman is resting her head on Atul's shoulder. She's smiling. Then Atul turns and kisses her on the lips. The couple is fastening their seat belts clearly in anticipation of the plane getting ready for takeoff.

Meera is confused.

"Listen," says Geeta. "Listen and watch."

Meera sees Atul's phone ring, and it's her name on the screen. He declines the call. Then he turns off his phone.

"Enough." Meera is shaken. But the puddle isn't done

"Who was that?" the woman asks Atul.

"Oh, some gold digger," he says. "She wants to marry me. Me? Imagine that. She was a fun fuck, but marriage?"

The Rain Maker

Geeta's story

There was no wedding.

Geeta knew and regretted not trusting her instincts. Her love for Dr. Meera had blinded her so much that she forgot to protect the doctor. Geeta had tried to will away her instinct in the hopes that Meera would be rewarded by good karma.

Of course, the Universe had its own plans. It always does.

Geeta sits at her assigned spot under the banyan tree inside the temple compound. She can feel her heart throbbing.

It was the moment that Meera made the comment about men not answering their phones. It was *that* specific moment Geeta's stomach had churned. She knew then that her instincts about the rich diamond man were right. She knew. She hated the fact that she would be the bearer of bad news for Meera. She had known that Damini was dead as well. Damini, her sister in pain, the healer, the giver of peace and serenity to tired humans. Her soul sister, Damini, was gone.

Geeta had met Damini a few years ago when she visited Shahajahanabad with Priest Prasad. Both the child and the woman knew what it was like to be bestowed with gifts they didn't desire. The gift she really wanted was the one that

Damini's sister, Yamini, had. The soul catcher, now *that* was a good gift, Geeta thought. With that gift, you give life. *With my gift, I only share the worst of human kind.* Geeta's thoughts race as she tries to find peace in her turbulent mind.

The red rain is now gone. The water is clear again. The puddles reflect the calm, still trees. Her mother arrives in waves of fury and leaves as gentle mist.

Geeta looks up at the sky and joins her palms together. She whispers thanks to the red rain. She ends her prayers with an appeal. "I hope Dr. Meera forgives me. I should have warned her earlier. Atul was an entitled man who was all about his life of luxury."

Geeta prays for another few minutes and heads towards the temple's inner sanctum. The red rain and the image had shaken Prasad and that surprised Geeta, because she considered him an ideal messenger of God; strong in his convictions, pure in his thoughts, respectful in his actions, and more than generous in his kindness. She stares at Prasad now as he sits on the stairs that lead to the main room. He looks even less composed than an hour ago.

"Priest Prasad, is everything okay? You look like you have seen a daayan," Geeta says.

Prasad places a finger on his lips, signaling Geeta to be silent for a moment.

"Yes. This is Priest Prasad calling. I need to report a death. I mean, I need to report an upcoming death—" He fumbles for the right words.

What on earth is he talking about? Geeta is stunned.

In an instant, it hits her. He saw something in a different

puddle of red rain. While Meera saw the truth, now it appears Prasad saw something as well.

Something so intense that he looked positively shaken.

"The rain only shows the truth, it cannot be used to stop anything. It is a mere mirror," she says again with quiet strength.

Prasad ends the call.

"But how do I live with what I know?" Prasad asks Geeta.

"I don't know. But the rain does. When the water visits again, I will ask her. The rain shows us many worlds and many truths that help us," Geeta whispers. Prasad places a hand on the girl's head. "You truly are a child of God," he says, and blesses her.

Chinmay, who has been out all morning, pushes Geeta aside.

"What is the matter?" he asks.

"Nothing. And everything. But God is really great and I will pray for a solution," Prasad says calmly.

Siya, the maid from a bungalow across the street, calls, "Geeta, Geeta come quick. Something is wrong with my Asha madam. She's not opening the door. Please come and help me."

Siya cooks, cleans, and takes care of the children who live there. She's about seventeen but looks less than ten years old and very frail. Siya doesn't normally panic like this, and although Geeta wants to ask her why, she holds her tongue.

Siya tugs at Geeta's hand.

Both girls run over and bang on the door.

"Asha madam, open this door. Asha madam, open this door now." Siya pounds on the wooden door and calls at the top of her lungs.

"Wait, Siya, move back a little," Geeta says.

Geeta places a palm on the door. She closes her eyes and

listens with her hands. She is one with the vibrations of the Universe and although she cannot see through the door, she can feel the presence of people inside. *Wait, there are many people inside, not just one.* Geeta jerks her hand back. There is no sound, no movement.

"Oh! Geeta, look at this, there's blood. Look, it appears to be coming up from the ground?" Siya panics as she sees deep red water gurgling up through the concrete tiles leading to the house. In a few seconds, the entire patio has stains of red as though someone has angrily flung paint on the ground.

Geeta looks and just for a moment is shaken. She didn't expect this. The red has, to date, only come from the sky. The fact that it's coming up from the ground is an omen. A really bad one.

"Siya, where are the children?" Geeta asks softly.

"The mean old daayan dadi took them to the vegetable market," Siya says, and her eyes become bigger. The daayan dadi, the grandmother sorceress, was Siya's way of referring to Asha's mother-in-law. The woman was grouchy, old, and even smelled evil. "She stinks of rotting flesh," Siya told Geeta once. "We had daayans in our village. Their feet don't touch the ground and they can shift shapes. Dadi isn't like a true daayan in form. But her spirit is more evil than all the daayans I know."

Siya adds now, "I don't know if they came back. I went to the laundry guy to give him the clothes to iron, so I don't know if they came back."

Geeta hates the daayan dadi too. In the deep of the night, when all else is quiet, she can hear the daayan dadi constantly screaming at her daughter-in-law and chiding her for not doing her work, not bringing in enough money, not being pretty enough for her son, Sundar.

Geeta places a palm on the door again.

Suddenly, the door opens, startling the two young girls.

"What are you two doing here? Get out of here!" The daayan dadi is standing there. "Siya, where are the clothes I told you to get ironed? Go get them and don't come back till you do. And you, what is your name? You, temple-cleaner girl? Get out of here. You have no business being here."

With that, she slams the door.

Siya comes close to Geeta and whispers, "Geeta, what should I do? I think something is wrong. Did you see her eyes? She looks like a maniac."

Geeta can feel Siya's shivering.

Geeta's hands have felt the vibrations of impending death—make that *deaths*—in the house.

"You go and get the clothes now, Siya. Let me see what I can do." No sense in having the girl witness the massacre happening inside.

Siya doesn't move. "Geeta, don't lie to me. If you know something, tell me now. I need to know."

Geeta stands still, unsure of what to do.

Siya is so fragile. She's been wearing the same green shirt and blue skirt for two years now. It's torn in places, restitched in others, and stained all over.

Geeta closes her eyes and tries to figure out what to do.

Her spirit answers.

Send her away to where she will be safe. You will never see her again. Your job is to protect the pure who live here. The pure like Dr. Meera. Like Asha madam. Your job is here.

"Siya, I need you to leave. Go to my spot under the banyan tree and dig. You will find some money. Take it all. Buy a ticket for The Pink City at the train station that's close to the big laundry. Take the 10:00 p.m. train. When you arrive in The Pink City, ask the man selling the guavas—his name is Raju Singh— ask him where Divya's sanctuary is. He will take you there. You will live there from now on. You will never have to worry about money or anything else ever again. I promise you."

Siya looks at the bloody water rising on the concrete. It's now seeping into the courtyard. The daayan dadi will be furious when she sees it. Instinctively Siya touches her arms. She can still feel the welts from the beating last week.

"But . . . but I can't leave you. I can't. She will beat you if I go," Siya says.

Geeta smiles. Siya is such a pure soul.

"At least I can save you today." Geeta hugs her friend.

"I will never be able to repay you," Siya says, distraught. "Save the children and Asha madam, please."

With that, she's gone.

The earth has swallowed up the sun and it's darker than hell now.

Geeta looks around. The normally busy street is empty. There's about an inch or so of water on the ground. She tries to stare at it carefully to see if there is a message, an image, a scene. Nothing. The water, at the moment, refuses to reveal anything.

Geeta goes to the side of the house and peers in through an open window.

The lights are on in the main hall and the kitchen.

The house is quiet.

Geeta hears whispers between a man and the daayan dadi.

The man, Geeta guesses, is the daayan dadi's son, Sundar, and Asha's husband. She has heard him before. Deep in the night when he rapes his wife, repeatedly. She knows his voice; a nasal tone dripping with self-entitlement.

Whimpering. Geeta hears whimpering.

She places a palm on the door again and closes her eyes.

She prays to her mother, The Goddess of Red Rain.

After a minute or so, she opens her eyes and bows to the red water at her feet.

"I'm ready," she says.

The whimpering is now loud. Very loud.

It's coming from the children. *They are alive.*

She wishes she could hear Asha madam's voice, but there's no sound from any woman other than the daayan dadi.

Geeta begins whispering, *This will not work if I am so anxious. I am here to do a job. I am not here to cry. My job is to help. Give me the strength, Mother.*

She moves quietly along the perimeter of the house to see if there is anything else open. Daayan dadi has closed all the large windows and doors. Geeta tries to gently move the screen on one of the windows. Nothing. She pushes another door. Nothing.

"Geeta, Asha madam once told me that there is a key inside the flowerpot in the back that opens the back door. I have never seen it, but I thought I would mention it. I . . . I have the money. I'm going,"

Geeta turns to see Siya standing behind her. She's holding Geeta's red pouch. Geeta places a finger on her lips and then signals for Siya to leave.

Hesitating, Siya turns and walks away from the only life she has ever known.

The flowerpot is right beside the door. Geeta sticks her hand in to see if she can find a key. Nothing. She tries the back door again. It is locked, but it's an old door.

Geeta goes back into the bushes and looks at the sky again.

She closes her eyes and holds her palms up to her Mother.

Red raindrops come pouring down, pounding the house, and within a matter of minutes, the rainwater surrounding the house begins to rise at a quicker pace.

The rainwater is her spy. It's going in to see what's going on. The water seeps in from the windows, from the front door, from the back door, from the ceiling.

Geeta has seen a lot of evil in her life. She has seen people being beaten, and dying of starvation in the streets, but nothing has prepared her for this.

The rain puddle shows her the inside of the house.

The two children and Asha madam are nude and sprawled on a sofa, foaming at the mouth. The daayan dadi and her son are sitting on another couch and smiling. Sundar, the father of these children and Asha madam's husband, is holding a knife.

"I can just start slicing them now. Why wait till they're dead?" he says.

"You are a stupid man. Do you know what happens when you cut a live person? They scream. They scream loudly. And if these worthless souls scream, we will have a crowd here in no time. The poison I gave them works slowly, but it's working. It's going to kill them soon. Then you can cut them up and take them to the garbage dump. There are dogs there that are always hungry. Now go get the plastic bags. Stupid Asha, getting pregnant with another girl. As if two granddaughters aren't shameful enough for me. You know how much I paid that doctor to tell me? Oh, what are you staring at me for—get the bags." The daayan dadi speaks firmly and with unquestionable authority.

Poison.

Geeta knows she needs to act now. It's time.

The rain stops. Its work is done, but the water is rising more, pushing against the back door.

"Open this door now or I will call the police," Geeta says loudly as she pounds on the wood. The sound of her voice echoes in the quiet of the night.

The door opens in an instant and the daayan dadi looks angry. A tiny woman wrapped in a dark purple saree, a red bindi on her forehead, thinning, white plaited hair—she looks like an overdressed, aging Indian soap star.

The daayan dadi, her perfectly white teeth glittering when she opens her mouth, stares at the red water seeping into the house. "What do you want? And what is this red water? What are you doing here?" Her eyes are wide with anxiety. She stomps her feet in the water and tries to push some of it out of the house.

Geeta shoves the old woman aside and steps inside. She turns around, looks up at the sky, smiles, and closes the door despite protests from the old woman.

"This is my house. You cannot just enter. I will call the police!"

"Please do. I think they would be very interested to see what is going on here." Geeta's response is calm, her voice steady.

In response, the old woman tries to punch Geeta, but Geeta

pushes her hard and moves towards the room the rain showed her.

The daayan dadi screams and curses. "Fine, you want to be in here, then you will meet the same fate as Asha and her cursed daughters."

The old woman tries to follow Geeta, but she discovers her feet won't move. Stunned, she looks down and yelps in fear that the red water has solidified around her ankles. No matter how hard she tries, she cannot free her feet.

Geeta's rain, the tears of her sweet Mother, has set hard as concrete.

The old woman won't be able to move. Ever.

Geeta goes to the back room where she has sensed the drama is unfolding.

Thankfully, the red rain has entered in time and reached the ankles of Sundar's feet.

Geeta sees Sundar sitting on the couch. He's screaming as he tries to stand and move, but the water won't let him, creating spikes and sharp shards around his feet. Each shard has the same poison he helped feed his children.

He sees Geeta and screams louder.

"You? The temple maid? Where is my mother? What did you do with her? What is the deal with this water? Make this stop or I will have you arrested. Do you know who I am?" Sundar is so angry he waves his hands in the air.

Geeta ignores him and goes to the little girls lying on the sofa. They are barely breathing. Asha madam is moaning. At least they're still alive.

The poor little girls' lips are turning blue.

Geeta breaks one of the pieces of the frozen red rain shards. She uses it to cut her finger. She places her finger on the lips of the first girl. She closes her eyes and life blood drips into the mouth of the dying child.

Instantly, the child begins to breathe, steadily now. Geeta does the same for the second girl, and then for Asha madam.

Geeta whispers to the rain around her, "I am filled now with all the evil that haunts us here on earth, oh Mother of mine. I am ready to take it all with me."

"Geeta? How did you do this? I—" Asha says, looking at Geeta and her children. Their eyes are open. The water has receded. They're safe now. Sundar is still on the couch, still screaming. Suddenly, he lurches forward to try to kill Asha with the knife. He falls on the poisonous shards.

"Asha madam, leave now. The rain will guide you."

Geeta's breathing stops before she can tell them that Asha madam and her beautiful daughters will now be the new rainmakers of this beautiful city.

Inside the temple sanctum, Priest Prasad sits, his eyes closed in prayers, hoping against hope that the vision in the puddle was fake.

He opens his eyes and looks at the ghee-lit lamp he has placed in front of the God's idol. He's about to stand when the flame goes out.

"No, no, no." Prasad sits back down. Sadness grips his heart. The vision has been realized—the red rain has taken her daughter home.

The Cleaning Lady

Siya's story

Siya can't sleep on the old train to The Pink City.

She sits, huddled, on a hard wooden seat and clutches the red pouch, her only worldly possession, close to her heart.

There are three other people in the train compartment. One is a sad-looking young woman with uncombed, purple-streaked hair, an old lady in blue, and a stout woman in white. Siya avoids eye contact with all of them.

"Where are you going, child? Are you alone?" the nice old lady in the blue dress asks. This is her fourth attempt at conversation.

Siya continues to look out the window instead of answering. She wants to tell them, *I am alone. I have always been alone. Yes, I am alone.*

The moon shimmers and throws silver light on the scene outside. Siya catches glimpses of ponds, huts, and, every now and again, a person walking in the night. It's raining again. She puts her hand out the window to check the color: water, plain, colorless water. The sensation of the water on her skin gives a strangely good feeling.

She closes her hand into a fist and feels good, relaxed.

Perhaps, Siya thinks, *this is Geeta's way of sending a message that all is well.*

The young woman with swollen eyes and puffed cheeks, who keeps running fingers through her purple-streaked hair, asks Siya, "Children your age shouldn't be traveling alone. Don't you have a family?"

"I have no one," Siya finally says.

The woman responds in a soft voice, "I have a little girl, my little Amya. She is much younger than you, but she is now lost. Lost to me, lost to this world."

"We don't know the ways of God. Only He knows why He does what He does," the woman in white says.

"Yes, blame it all on a God, who none of us even know exists. How is this fair to this young girl or this woman who cries for her lost child?"

The crying woman curls up into a ball and closes her eyes.

Siya shivers and closes her window.

"Do you want some poori aloo?" the lady in blue asks Siya as she holds out some bread. The train compartment smells like when Asha madam cooks—aromas of fried potatoes laced with garlic and cumin, the sweet smell of yogurt with cucumber and cilantro, and the pooris.

"I have a little money. How much?" Siya asks as she looks longingly at the food. The money in the red pouch is too precious to waste on food, but she's hungry. She hasn't eaten all day. The daayan dadi only allowed her one meal a day, and that was yesterday afternoon. Asha madam used to slip her extra food on the sly, but they were caught once and beaten, so there had been no more secret exchanges recently.

"No, no, no money. Just eat, child. You look like you haven't eaten in days." The lady offers Siya the poori.

Siya accepts and greedily bites into the fried bread.

The old lady offers food to the other women in the compartment. The woman with the glorious purple hair, who is softly weeping for her child, refuses.

"How can I eat when I have lost everything? My child, my husband—" The woman tries to wipe away tears.

The old lady has a soft, soothing voice. "I'm so sorry about your family. I don't know who you are or where you are from, but my mother used to say we should never refuse food or walk away from it. It is an insult to the Gods who are sharing this abundance with us. Here, have a sip of this water and eat. Soon we'll be in The Pink City, the city of blessings for all, and all will be well."

The young grief-stricken woman takes a bite. Then she opens a pendant she's wearing and shows Siya and the old lady a picture of her young daughter and husband.

"All will be well. The Pink City is the land of blessings," the old woman says, and then launches into a song that extols the virtues of The Pink City.

Siya eats her food, drinks the water, listens to the lady singing the quiet lullaby, and at some point falls asleep.

The stout old lady in white shrieks and points to Siya. "Look, oh dear God, she is a *devil* child."

Everyone looks. There are shards of red glass surrounding Siya, who is oblivious to them. The complaining passenger huddles closer to the others. Fear-tinged sweat pours down her cheeks.

The lady in blue says, "She is not evil. She is the child of the Goddess, and the Goddess is protecting her. Don't you see? She is a little baby, traveling alone. What would have happened if there were wicked men in this compartment? Or thieves? Or anyone else with intentions to harm her? She is being protected. Go to sleep and let her rest." With that, she begins her song again.

The grief-stricken young mother smiles for the first time. She hasn't smiled in days. "Yes, God protects the ones He loves. But sometimes we need the evidence to have the faith."

***

There's no trace of anything unusual around Siya as the morning sun beams into the compartment, warming it instantly.

The old lady gently pats Siya's shoulder. "Wake up, little girl, your station is here."

"Here? We are here? Thank you for waking me and for the meal." Siya gets up and holds the woman's hands.

"No thanks needed. This is what we are here for, right? To help each other?" The lady takes her bags and moves towards the exit. "Take care of yourself, little girl, you are the Goddess's gift to us."

The grief-stricken lady also gets out on the same platform. She looks around and then sits on a wooden bench.

There are very few people at this early hour and the smell of ginger tea fills the morning air. A few vendors are setting up their carts and stray passengers are asleep on the benches. Siya looks around and tries to recall the name of the vendor Geeta told her to contact. She can't remember and now she's in this new city with nowhere to go. She looks to see if the lady in blue is still around, but she's long gone.

The lady with purple hair, sitting on the bench, is simply staring at the sky.

Siya goes over to a vendor selling tea, buys a cup, and takes it to the lady with purple hair. "Please, drink this. I know you haven't eaten. I will pray that the Goddess will help you with your child."

The lady takes the cup of tea and smiles a feeble smile.

Siya says goodbye and heads back to a bench and sits down. *Why can't I remember? Why am I so stupid? What was his name—? *She looks around for a sign, but it's futile. She doesn't even know what she's looking for.

A vendor sings from his cart just behind Siya's bench. "Mangoes, bananas, guavas . . . come get fruit for your trip. It will never give you a stomachache, and will make your sweetheart love you more."

Siya jumps up. Guava, didn't Geeta say go to the man selling guavas? Or was it grapes? She decides to ask.

"Are you . . . are you Geeta's friend? She sent me here. She said you could help me. Do you know her?"

The thin, short man singing the praises of his fruit stops and stares at the young girl.

"Get away from here and don't spoil my morning business. If people see you here, no one will come buy my fruits. Now go away, shoo!" With that he begins to call out loud the benefits of mangoes. Then he whispers, "What is your proof she sent you?"

Siya wonders what to do. She has no proof. She goes back to the bench and spots the red pouch. How could she have forgotten that?

She returns to the man selling fruit.

"I have proof. I have this. She gave me this before she told me to come here—to go to . . . I remember now, Divya's sanctuary. She said a man at the station selling guavas would take me there. See this, she gave me this." Siya knows she's in the right place, talking to the right man.

The man stares at the pouch, and suddenly his demeanor goes from happy to sad. He says nothing but places his hand on Siya's head. He signals to a young boy sitting beside his cart to watch it and, holding Siya's hand, leads her outside the station.

"Geeta sent you to the right place. I will help you."

"Where is Divya's sanctuary? Also, what is it? Will I be safe there? Please tell me something. Why are you crying? I don't understand. Please tell me *something*," Siya pleads. The man says nothing more and walks fast, still holding Siya's hand and staring straight ahead.

The hot sun beats down on the morning traffic, now in full throttle assailing their senses with harsh fumes and loud horns.

"Walk fast or we'll miss Divya. She will be out soon," the man says. He pulls her along to match his pace.

Siya jerks her hand away and stops.

"I'm not going anywhere with you until you tell me who you are, where we are going, and why you're crying. I will *not* move."

He turns to see Siya standing still. Her hands are trembling, but she looks determined.

"Geeta knows a pure soul when she sees one." He manages a smile.

"Keep talking."

"My name is Raju. I'm a messenger between people like Geeta, who we believe are angels, and the sanctuary where people

159

like her send souls they think need help, or can help others. Happy now? I'm not telling you anything else until you start walking and, of course, tell me your name."

"My name is Siya," Siya says as she breaks into a short run to keep up with Raju, who has already reached the end of the footpath.

"See that? That big area with the fence? That is where Divya lives. She runs a home for the homeless. Her job is collecting people no one wants. The ones who have been debilitated by poverty, illness, life, and sometimes even family. She finds them on the street, in the gutters; the beggars and the lost all have a home here. She offers food, education, and more importantly, shelter from the world outside. Some even make it out and find a new life for themselves. Most just find a safe place to die," he says and helps Siya cross the busy street to the entrance. The name on the board reads ASTHA, hope.

As Raju and Siya reach the entrance, the wooden door opens and a tall, dark-complexioned, slim lady steps out. She's dressed from head to toe in yellow. Her long, flowing black hair is open and casually pulled over one shoulder. Her glow rivals that of the sunshine.

Raju folds his hands and greets the woman, "Namaste, Divya."

"Raju? I didn't expect you here today. And who is this sweet little guest you bring with you?" Divya bends down and pinches Siya's cheeks. Then she looks up at Raju, who points to the red pouch that Siya is gripping so tightly.

"No, no," Divya says sadly.

"What's going on here? I need to know. What have I done?

Why are *you* crying when you see me? First him and now you. I've not harmed anyone. What are you crying for?" Siya places her hands on her hips and stands as tall as she can.

"I know I need to explain, but first tell me why Geeta sent you here," Divya asks in a gentle, kind voice.

Siya explains quickly and with as little drama as possible. She still doesn't trust these two adults.

"Oh, so you are the truth seeker? You were seeking the truth about your employer, about Raju, and now about me. Geeta certainly sent us a good spirit." With that Divya places her hand on Siya's head.

"From this day forward, you will always get the truth you seek. Your heart and your spirit are pure. No truth will remain hidden from you," Divya says. "Your name here will be Jigyasa, the curious one. The seeker of all truths."

Siya stands there.

"I will *not* let you change my name or give me any kind of blessing until you tell me why you are all crying. I feel like I've done something wrong." The long journey, losing the only home she has ever known, and now these strangers wanting to change her name—are too much for Siya to take.

"It's not you." Divya stares at Raju, her dark brown eyes pleading for support.

"It's not good, dear child. But since you're now the truth seeker, we have no choice," Raju says.

"Child, come here." Divya pulls Siya close and hugs her.

Siya stiffens. It's her first real compassionate, human touch.

Divya says, "Whenever Geeta sends us someone, they always carry a pouch. She makes sure they have enough money to get here and for anything else they may need. You don't know this, but that money pouch will never run out for you. It will clothe you and feed you as long as your heart remains pure."

Divya takes Siya—now Jigyasa—into the compound. Raju follows quietly.

Jigyasa looks around the enormous complex. There are open rooms all along the periphery. Some rooms are filled with children who are sitting in classrooms of sorts. Others reveal old people on beds. Two have women doing needle work. On one side, several people are cooking in a kitchen. There are cows, deer, dogs, and cats milling around.

Jigyasa turns her attention back to Divya.

"I didn't know that about the pouch. She didn't say anything."

Divya smiles. "No, she never would tell you that. That is my job. The reason we are crying . . . you see, usually the pouches she sends are green. That's a sign that all is well. The pouch you are carrying is red—"

Raju adds quietly, "Geeta is now one with her rain. She's no longer of this earth."

Jigyasa stands still. She folds her hands and looks up to the sky. "Thank you, Geeta, my friend, my savior, for everything. I promise to work and help as many as I can. Just as you have helped me."

Divya's reaction is euphoric. "Oh, child. You see? You *are* the truth seeker. The truth doesn't hurt you. In your case, it sets you free. And through you now, it will set others free."

They continue through the compound and Divya keeps talking.

"You know, the locals call me the cleaning lady. They say I clear their streets of the children of poor luck. My job is to bring them here, to try and heal them. It's not easy, this work. All the people that Geeta sends my way help here. They teach, they cook, they clean, they try to make the world a little less hellish for these poor souls."

Jigyasa can't imagine a better place to be. The air is filled with peace, the energy of this little city inside The Pink City promises hope. Jigyasa smiles as a kitten comes up to nuzzle her leg.

"Now come, I will show you your living space. It's small, but it's yours. Bathe and get ready, there is much to do. The girls here will give you some clothes and then we must be going. I needed help today, and it looks like the spirits knew just who to send."

They hear muffled screams coming from one of the rooms.

"Oh, who is that? Sounds like she's in a lot of pain," Jigyasa says. Then she suddenly stops in front of the door. "I feel like I need to give the person in this room a message. But I'm not sure what that even means. What's happening to me? I don't know who's in there, and I don't know what the message is or *how* I know these things."

Divya says, "All I can tell you is the one thing that I've learned in life: faith before fear."

Jigyasa isn't even sure what that means. "Who is in there?"

Divya hesitates. Yamini doesn't like visitors.

163

The Truth Seeker

Jigyasa's story

Everyone at Astha is shuffling towards the temple this morning. Jigyasa, who has been pretty much eating and sleeping in her room for a week now, finally decides to join the world outside.

The only sounds are from the children who are running fast and singing a silly song about feet and tails. The cows that have been mooing incessantly all morning are, finally, asleep. The crows are quiet—thank God for small mercies—and nowhere to be seen.

The sunrise prayers are just beginning and Jigyasa pushes to the front of the crowd at the temple.

The "temple" consists of a grassy area that has been cleared to accommodate an idol of the elephant god, Ganesh. Surrounding His statue are several pots of roses and a few pots of jasmine. One of Divya's rescues, an old beggar, performs the prayers. He knows the prayers perfectly. He won't reveal how he knows them, but rumor has it that he fell in love with a priest and the temple authorities beat him black and blue and left him to rot on the streets. Divya found him in a ditch, covered with fecal matter and urine.

As the entire group gathers for morning prayers, the girls tell

Jigyasa that the day always begins with Divya making them say a gratitude prayer.

"Oh, there is one thing that is especially wonderful in the morning," one of the girls tells Jigyasa. It is the prasadam—the blessed food offered to the worshippers. Every day it's different, and today it is a terra cotta bowl filled with rice pudding.

"This is how the rich atone their sins—they feed us," Divya whispers as she passes out the pudding. She then waves to a gentleman sitting in his imported car just outside the complex. He waves back. The girls tell Jigyasa the man is the donor of the day.

"Divya, how is the woman in the room? The one who was screaming the other day? I can't stop thinking about her," Jigyasa asks.

"I think it is time for you to meet her. Come with me," Divya says.

Jigyasa stands in front of the room listening to the noises coming from inside. She hesitates but then opens the door. The woman is clearly in pain as she twists and turns.

"What do you want? Who are you? Where is Divya?" the woman asks.

Divya introduces them. "Jigyasa, this is my cousin Yamini." Yamini is in the shadows, the room is dark, and she warns them about turning on any lights because they hurt her eyes.

"What is wrong with you?" Jigyasa asks.

"I don't know. Something went wrong. I was trying to save someone and help them. But I—I don't have any vision. I don't know where to go. I'm burdened with this soul. It is killing me. I don't know where to go," Yamini says through her groans.

"I don't know how to help. But I have a feeling . . . although I'm not sure. I will return," Jigyasa says, and asks Divya to close the door.

"Go, go to hell. No one ever helps me," Yamini yells.

"Jigyasa, don't worry about her. But child, you will have to come help me today." Divya gently tousles the child's beautiful hair.

Jigyasa shuffles her feet nervously. "Can't I just stay inside? I don't want to go back out."

"You're a silly girl. Go get dressed and meet me at the gate in a few minutes. Oh, and by the way, I told Raju to keep an eye out for your grief-stricken lady. He called a few minutes ago to say that someone had spotted her at the train station again. Your description of her purple hair was perfect. I will see if I can find out more. Okay? Now go get ready."

Jigyasa trudges back to her room, a place she shares with four other girls. She has her own mattress, a set of drawers, three full set of clothes, two pairs of slippers, a comb, and underwear. By her own standards, she is wealthy beyond belief.

"Why the long face? What is wrong?" asks a roommate.

"Divya wants to take me with her. I hate the world outside. I hate it and I don't want to go." Jigyasa sits down on the mattress and begins to bite her nails.

One of the young girls, with only one good leg, ambles slowly towards Jigyasa and places an arm around her shoulder. "Divya will never let anything happen to you. Look at me. See this belly? This baby is coming any time. My mother threw me out when *her* boyfriend did this to me. Divya has helped you stay here and be safe. Now, it's your turn to return that favor."

"Oh, I see. So this place is like any other. You scratch my back and I scratch yours?" Jigyasa mumbles. Then she begins to weep. "I don't want this life of always being obligated to someone. I just want to be free."

"You are being silly."

The voice, loud and gruff and full of authority, belongs to Aryan, one of the few young men in the compound. He is the tallest, most handsome man Jigyasa has ever seen and she quickly pulls herself together as he enters.

"Stop crying. When you cry like this and feel sorry for yourself, you're insulting us all. You're no longer a victim. None of us are. We are now, thanks to Divya, empowered to help others. Now stop weeping like a baby. Get dressed and go with her. When you come back, we will all sit together and we can chat and talk. You know, like a real family. Deal?"

"Yes, deal." Jigyasa is awestruck. The mere thought of spending time with this handsome man prompts Jigyasa to stop crying.

In an instant Jigyasa goes from not wanting to leave to wanting to run out and experience the adventure so that she can come back and tell Aryan all about it.

"Good girl. Do you know what I have to do all day?" he says. "I will be cooking. So you have a more adventurous day ahead of you than I do."

Dressed in a violet shirt and a black skirt, Jigyasa feels like a princess. She's grateful for the embroidered slippers that a rich donor gave all the residents of Astha. She takes a few steps. Her mind can't comprehend that nothing cuts, nothing slices, nothing pierces her feet. Oh, the joys of wearing footwear.

"Jigyasa, I am thrilled you'll join me. Now we have to rush to the train station," Divya says. They leave the compound.

"Why are we going there?" Jigyasa asks as fear creeps back in.

Divya doesn't answer, staring ahead.

The residents of The Pink City are up and about as they go about their daily routines. The noisy roads are filled with bike and bullock carts, cars and buses, and of course a sea of countless people on foot as they navigate the overflowing city streets. Jigyasa sees Hawa Mahal, the legendary palace where queens spent their leisure time.

A skinny vendor standing with his nearly disintegrating cart calls out, "Divya, Divya, come drink some coconut water. It will cool you off on this hot day."

Divya stops at the cart, which is parked precariously on the edge of the major street that forms an artery of the city. Cars and buses whiz by unbelievably close, but the young man doesn't seem concerned.

"I don't think we have time today. We have to get to the—" The loud siren of a police van drowns out the rest.

The police van stops behind the cart and a stout officer steps out.

Jigyasa moves behind Divya and tries to hide. The coconut vendor hands Jigyasa a coconut, top sliced off, with a straw. "You drink this. It will give you good energy."

The policeman's pockmarked face scrunches into a grimace. "Divya, this one is the worst I have ever seen. I don't even know what to tell you." He pulls out a white handkerchief to wipe the sweat dribbling down both sides of his face. His deputy, still sitting in the car, calls out to him.

"Sir, the buzzards are approaching the body. The train station master has called again to tell us to hurry up."

Divya, Jigyasa, and the policeman get in the van. The deputy races towards the train station.

"Damn this traffic," the policeman says again and again.

"Divya, what is going on? A body?" Jigyasa asks.

Divya simply pats her hand and says, "You are going where your spirit can help us the most."

The train station has five policemen posted at the front gate. There are people complaining about being late for their trains, but the police refuse to let them in. The crowd gets louder as they see the police van approach.

The policeman calls out, "As you know, we have had a major crime committed in this area. For those of you complaining that it's delaying your trip, what if this was your family? Would you still want me to let everyone in to destroy the evidence?" The crowd hushes up.

Divya takes Jigyasa's hand and steps out of the van. Jigyasa pulls back.

"It's okay, I promise no harm will come to you. You are here to serve, not be hurt," Divya says gently.

Jigyasa hesitatingly walks behind Divya, following her into the mostly empty train station.

Divya takes out her phone and sends a message to Aryan. *I NEED YOU HERE. NOW.*

Apart from a stray police officer, the only signs of life in the train station are the sounds of buzzards and barking dogs in the distance.

Divya and Jigyasa move towards the sounds. The policeman

169

trails behind them. Far ahead, they can see three men dressed in green standing beside the train tracks. Two of them are using poles to fend off the dogs. One is trying to shoo the buzzards away.

"Death is in the air," Jigyasa whispers. She stops as she feels an urgent need well up inside her.

Suddenly, she lets go of Divya's hand and runs towards the men in green. She stops when she reaches the blood-smeared tracks. There are the remnants of a couple of human bodies on the tracks: mutilated hands, a torn leg, part of a head smashed in, a foot wearing a red shoe.

Jigyasa takes in the scene. Divya quickly catches up. The dogs leave, and the vultures fall silent.

"There was a baby," Jigyasa says. "One man, one woman, both are dead. But where is the baby?"

"A baby?" Divya asks.

The policeman says to Divya, pointing to the far side of the tracks, "How did you know about the baby? The baby is safe. Not a single bruise. We sent her to the hospital anyway. See that woman there, on the side of the tracks? She was the one holding onto the baby."

Divya's eyes turn towards the woman, and she quickly bends to Jigyasa to tell her what she sees, but Jigyasa is on the side of the tracks, throwing up. The sight of the mutilated bodies is too much.

As the policeman explains the situation, Aryan arrives.

Jigyasa looks flustered and says, "Why am I here? This is what you wanted me to see? They are not even there anymore, what can I do to help?"

Divya puts her arm around Jigyasa. "Child, you will help, but you needed to see where it all ended before we can find out where it all began. Now, let's try it again. Look at the scene, what do you see? Look *inside* you, and you will find the truth."

Divya has been waiting for this truth seeker to arrive. Their last one left her body for heaven a few months ago. It was time for a new seeker and Divya knows that if Jigyasa centers her energy, she will be able to see the truth.

Divya herself no longer wishes to seek the truth. Divya only cleans, having once told Aryan, "I just want to believe in the fairytale. I don't care to know the truth anymore. It hurts too much."

Jigyasa stares around for a minute and then closes her eyes. In her heart, she asks Geeta to show her the truth. Jigyasa's mind settles, her heartbeat becomes steady, and she becomes still. A sense of calm comes over her. A fuzzy image slowly unfolds in her mind's eye: She sees one woman running on the tracks holding a baby. The baby is crying, and the woman is running fast. The woman's leg gets stuck in the track and she falls down. Still holding the baby.

"Oh, God," Jigyasa begins to tremble. But she breathes deeply. Instinctively, she reaches out to help the woman who has fallen. The wind blows and the scene shimmers as if with anger. The image Jigyasa is seeing is gone. She looks at Divya or Aryan for support, but they are both standing quietly, eyes closed, hands folded in prayer.

Guide me, Geeta. Show me what happened. Show me the truth.

Jigyasa tries to see who else is there, who they are running from, but that is a blur. Then she sees a new scene. A man

171

walking by the tracks sees the two people—a woman and a baby—on the tracks and rushes to help them. He picks up the baby and wonders what to do. He sees another woman on the side and gives her the baby and tells her to move away from the tracks. Then he turns back to the woman on the tracks. A train approaches, but he isn't able to move off the track in time. He and the woman are torn apart and die on impact. Jigyasa is about to open her eyes to tell them what she has seen: There was no murder, here but a brutal accident. But something tugs at her soul. *Is there more, Geeta?*

Breathe, breathe, Geeta will guide me. There is more.

Clear as day, suddenly Jigyasa sees the woman with the purple hair sitting by the side of the tracks holding the baby. The woman is rocking the baby back and forth and singing a song, and then says, "Trains aren't good for children. Trains can hurt children. I will protect you."

Jigyasa opens her eyes and tells them what she has seen.

The policeman gives the three men a signal and they begin picking up whatever body parts they can and placing them in polyethylene bags.

"Jigyasa, are there any marks on the woman's body?" Aryan asks.

"What kind of a question is that?"

"There are a lot of junkies here. I just want to see if there is anything on her body we can use to find out who she is."

Jigyasa closes her eyes again. She tells them what she sees: There are two tattoos on the woman's arms. One of a butterfly, and one of a lotus.

Aryan says, "Oh God, that is Shanti. Then the baby wasn't

hers. She has no children. I know you will think I'm cruel for saying this, but in so many ways she is better off dead. I'm glad the baby is safe."

"Better off killed under a train?" Jigyasa doesn't hide her disgust. "And the man who tried to save her? He saved the baby but died in such a cruel way."

Aryan shakes his head and says, "She was barely alive when she lived. She was completely addicted to whatever it is that was new on the market. She stole for it, gave her body up for it, and in the end must have died for it. I do feel sorry for the man who tried to save her. I'm not heartless. And the baby is fine."

"Your new girl here is good. Very good. She is correct about the man. And I will ask my boys to check the tattoos," the policeman says, and pulls out a roti stuffed with onions and green chilies, and begins to eat. Nothing fazes him anymore. *Why miss breakfast? Humans don't deserve humanity.*

"Do we know anything about the baby?" Divya asks.

"No one we called knows why or how she had a newborn with her. My staff has already checked the three local hospitals. No reports of any missing newborns, but we will keep looking."

Divya asks, "Jigyasa, the woman that was holding the baby, is that the same woman who was in the train with you? Not too many women here have purple hair."

The policeman looks confused "Purple hair? She was sitting right there. I just pointed her out to you. Now where is she?"

"I feel like I need to help her," Jigyasa says, and suddenly becomes agitated. A quick search proves futile, the woman is long gone.

The policeman signals to his men and they begin clearing the

173

tracks and filling the body bags. "We will call you later for the cremation. Now, we go and get all this analyzed."

At Jigyasa's insistence, Aryan continues to search for the woman with purple hair but to no avail.

Just as they are getting ready to leave, Aryan tells them to stop.

"Look there," he says, pointing to a woman sitting outside the train station on the footpath.

"It's her. I need to talk to her," says Jigyasa, and without waiting for anyone runs over.

The sounds coming out of the woman's mouth are like an animal in pain. Aryan follows Jigyasa. The woman doesn't move. She stops crying and stares at a bottle of water Aryan offers. Instead of drinking it, she pours it on her head, places her face in her hands and begins to weep.

"You found my girl? Is she okay?" the woman asks them.

"The baby you saved is fine. Who are you?" Aryan asks.

"I . . . I am Sehar. You found my daughter? Is she okay? My little girl. She is on the train."

"Sehar, my name is Aryan. Do you know where you are?"

Sehar starts to shake, and she looks around. "I don't know where I am. What is this place?"

"Aryan. My name is Aryan."

A train pulls into the station and startles all of them.

Sehar sees the train and her face turns white. "My daughter. Oh, my God. That train. My Amya."

"Here take this, it will help you calm down." Aryan, noticing the tobacco stains on her teeth, offers her a cigarette and really hopes that she will take it.

Jigyasa says, "Do you remember me? From the train? Take it. Please? These are good people."

Sehar hesitates. And then something makes her take a whiff of the cigarette. It takes a few minutes and she relaxes. Aryan introduces her to Divya and they all sit down next to her, waiting for her mind to settle.

"Rishi, my husband, was diagnosed with pancreatic cancer a few months ago. His health was failing rapidly and he no longer wished to live. He wanted to die on the Nirvana Train."

"Wait, what? He wanted to die on a train? I am not sure I understand," Divya says.

"It's a euthanasia train that was built to help people like him commit painless suicide. We were . . . I mean, is there such a thing as painless suicide? He was acting insane. We were in the waiting room. The three of us. Rishi, me, and my little girl, Amya. Oh, poor Amya—" Sehar begins to cry but keeps talking. "I kept telling him I needed him and he couldn't just kill himself. We would fight his illness. Just as he and I were talking, Amya, my baby, got in the carriage and the train departed."

Aryan, Divya, and Jigyasa gasped together, looking at each other, unsure of what to say.

"Why didn't someone stop the train?" Jigyasa says.

"Train is really not the right word for it. It's more like a few compartments that move at lightning speed and kill whatever is inside. There is no brake, no emergency stop, nothing. Once you get on, it is all over. Amya was on the train. All I remember after that is that I ran out of that place. I just ran and ran, I don't know how long it has been."

Sehar quietly adds, "It's all my fault. I'm the mother. I should have protected her. I let her get on that train and now you tell me I have caused problems here? I am so sorry."

"Everything is fine here. How long have you been away from your home? Have you contacted them? They must be so worried," Divya says.

Sehar looks unsure of what to do. The glazed look in her eyes returns.

Divya asks her, "Sehar, do you want to call your husband? He must be so worried."

"Call? Oh? I don't have my phone. I—I don't want to know what has happened." They convince Sehar to contact home and watch as she makes a video call. "Wait what? I don't believe it! What? No, no . . . please God, no . . . Yes, Rishi, I am okay," Sehar stares at the screen.

"What happened?" Divya asks gently.

"I thought my little girl had died on that train, but Rishi says Amya is still alive, but barely. I thought all this time the train had killed her, but she is hanging on . . . Amya *is* dying. I—I . . . They are my life. What will I do without them? I love them . . . here, see?"

Sehar turns the screen towards Divya.

Divya lets out a gasp. "Wait. Wait. What is your husband's full name?" He is barely recognizable, but she needs to be sure.

"Huh? My family is dying and you want to know about my husband?"

"Please tell me his name? Your full name? Is he Rishi Khanna who went to Delhi University? Lives in Shahajahanabad? You are Sehar Khanna?" Divya asks, stunned.

"Yes."

Before Divya can ask anything else, Jigyasa says, "Sehar, I need a photo of Amya right now."

"What? What is wrong with you both? First his name, now her photo."

"I don't have time to explain. I need to see her photo to be sure."

Jigyasa had a vision earlier in the day, but it had been fuzzy. Sehar pulls up a family photo that is on a website. As soon as the photo comes up on the phone, Jigyasa is sure. This is the one.

"Get up, Sehar. Let's go. I know someone who can help Amya."

The Soul Catcher Returns

Yamini's story

"Why do you lie to me? No one can save Amya. The man who created the train told us." Sehar's tone is icy and she stares at Jigyasa with obvious contempt.

Aryan says, "You don't know everything. There are those who can heal beyond what the humans can see or feel or touch. The truth seeker has seen something and if your little girl is still breathing, we can try to save her."

He turns around and breaks into a run towards the parking lot. Sehar is unsure at first and then with Divya's help follows Aryan to the Jeep. Divya loads Sehar onto the back and gets in the front.

"Let's go to Astha, and then we'll head to Shahajahanabad."

Outside, the night is chilly. The rain is still beating down anything that comes in its way. The only sound is the water swooshing on the sides of the street as the odd car goes by. The Jeep cuts across alleyways and takes a dark, short road that comes out directly in front of Astha.

The Jeep pulls in.

Divya is sharp and direct. "I want to make one thing clear. When you go in to see her, you only discuss Amya. Is that clear?

You don't mention anyone else. Do you understand me? If you do, you will lose your chances of saving your child. You get one shot at this."

Aryan and Jigyasa look confused but say nothing.

Sehar nods. "I will do anything to save her."

The rain slows down, the clouds have cleared, and the stars begin to twinkle. Sehar looks around the compound and sees most people are sleeping on their cots under tents. Lanterns hanging on ropes crisscross the compound giving it a celebratory appearance.

"Aryan, where am I?" Sehar whispers.

Divya says, "Let me explain. I am Divya. I run this facility. It is a home for all the gentle people in the world that could not fit into a regular society."

They come to a closed door. Sehar can see a white light spilling under it onto the concrete, and the gentle sounds of flute music can be heard.

"Yamini is an angel. Angels always help. But she is very ill. She hasn't said a word in a week," Divya says.

"Yamini? Wait, Yamini is here? The soul catcher? Oh, no. I know of her. She will never help us. My husband nearly destroyed her," Sehar says.

"This is why you won't tell her who you are. Do you want to save your daughter or not?"

Jigyasa says, "Yamini and I spoke this morning. Since her sister's death, she has been having trouble receiving her visions. She told me she has to save someone, but the guidance isn't coming through. She asked me to help. I kept seeing a fuzzy image. Then I saw the photo of your daughter. That is whom she has to save. She told me to bring you here. She gives life, Sehar. She *gives* life."

The door opens, the music stops, and a singsong voice says, "Please send her in. We don't have time."

Sehar rushes inside. An overheard lamp shines brightly. There are incense sticks making the place smell of roses and frangipani.

"Come in. I have been expecting you. Shut the door behind you."

Sehar closes the door and goes to the woman on the bed. A beautiful round face, framed by cascades of black wavy hair, gleaming eyes, and a glittering smile are not what Sehar is expecting. The woman is covered in a red blanket from head to toe.

"I have been waiting for you." Yamini manages a smile.

"Can you help me? Please? My child is dying." Sehar is already pleading.

The wind blows through an open window.

"Yes, I can help you, but in return, you will have to do as I ask. You can't question me and you can't change your mind. I will give you what you ask for, but you will *have* to give me what I want in return. Think about it. I give you five minutes."

"I don't need to think. I will give you anything. I will give you my life in exchange for Amya's. I promise. Please, let's go."

Sehar is already up and at the door waiting for Yamini.

"Nothing is as easy as it seems. I have your word, yes? If not, remember I can take back what I have given, and it will not be pretty."

Sehar impatiently opens the door. "Please, let's go. She doesn't have much time. If she makes it through this night, it will be a miracle."

Yamini removes the blanket and Sehar lets out a scream. Yamini's legs are rotting. The flesh has burns, but there is no blood, no smell.

"This is a long story. Don't worry, I'm not contagious, just helpless. When Aryan drives, the road becomes shorter. We will get there before the sunrise. Ask Divya to find a wheelchair. Oh, and take that bag, the one in the corner. It has my candles."

Sehar picks up the black handbag.

"I'll tell Aryan and Divya," she says and opens the door.

Divya is already waiting with a wheelchair.

"We are ready. Aryan is getting the Jeep."

Sehar and Divya try to lift Yamini off the bed and onto the wheelchair. It takes every drop of strength from both. Divya finally calls for some of the young men in the compound to help.

Sehar says, "She is so tiny, how can she be so heavy?"

"This is the story of my life," Yamini says faintly.

They quickly push the wheelchair over the muddy, wet grass and towards the Jeep. The men help move Yamini to the back seat, then fold her wheelchair and are about to put it in the back when she says, "Don't. I won't be needing that after this ride."

Divya raises an eyebrow but knows better than to ask Yamini any questions.

They get in the car and Aryan asks Sehar where they need to go. He says, "Based on this weather and the roads, I think I can get us there in under five hours. Let me try."

The Jeep zooms through the dark night. The passengers sit in a silence no one seems to want to break. The breeze is chilly, with the scent of frangipani that accompanies Yamini wherever she goes.

"Sehar, all will be well." Yamini places a hand on Sehar's head.

The landscape blurs as Aryan speeds up. There are a few trucks on the road, but no other traffic. The Gods have cleared the way to help a dying soul.

"You cry because you don't have faith," Yamini says to Sehar.

Sehar sighs, "I fear her brain may be gone already."

As he hits the brakes to bring the Jeep back to a regular speed, Aryan says, "We should be there in about ten more minutes. I will need to slow down now."

A gentle sun is rising and begins to spread a glow to the earth. The sky is moving from shades of black and grey to hues of gold and blue. Several white clouds dot the great blue expanse. People are waking up and the roads are starting to fill with cars, motorcycles, and buses. At several points Aryan notices schoolchildren standing and waiting at bus stops.

"The house is on the right after the next turn," Sehar says anxiously. "I hope we made it in time."

Aryan pulls up in front of a two-story bungalow. The balconies are filled with pots of blooming roses. Several towels are hanging out to dry on a clothesline on the second floor. Sehar gets out of the Jeep and runs to the main door to ring the bell. Aryan tells Divya to follow.

"I'll bring Yamini. You go in and see what is going on."

A young man dressed in a white T-shirt and jeans opens the door. "Sehar? You have returned. She is barely there. Come quick. You must say goodbye." He pulls her into the house.

Divya follows quietly with Aryan, who is carrying a whimpering Yamini. Her face, which normally glows and lights up with life, grimaces with each breath.

They find themselves in a cozy house filled with photographs of a smiling young girl and a handsome couple. Toys are scattered on the couches and tables. The smell of medication fills the air.

"Death is almost here. Hurry," Yamini says.

The bedroom is small but airy. All the windows are open. On the bed, a little girl is lying still. Next to her is Rishi. His face is ashen and his breathing is shallow.

Sehar kisses her daughter and sits by Rishi's side holding his hand.

Yamini comes in and looks at Amya. Yamini is about to say something when she sees the man on the bed.

It can't be. Rishi? No, it can't be. The one who took everything away from me. The one who destroyed my life? That Rishi? Fate is cruel.

Yamini is stunned. The pain shoots through her body. She realizes she doesn't have much time.

She looks at his face again. The love of her life. There is death around him. Rishi is dying. His eyes are closed. His breathing is labored. He's almost ready to leave. Yamini looks unsure of what do to.

"Rishi? You are Rishi's wife? Amya is Rishi's child? He is dying . . . *she* is dying."

Sehar says, "Please save *her*. She is a child. She has her whole life in front of her. She is only a baby. He is dying. I know he will be gone soon. If he was awake, I know he would want you to save his only child."

Yamini looks out a window to get a peek at the sky. *Give me strength to make the right decision. To choose the right one. Two of them are dying. The love of my life. My love, my heartbreak. My soulmate, my betrayer. And the love of his life. This baby. Oh, Mother. What should I do?*

Everything fades into the background. Yamini stares intently at the sky. There is a twinkle. The soul catcher knows exactly what she needs to do.

Yamini tells Sehar, "Come here. Remember I told you I will ask you for something. I am ready." Yamini whispers something to Sehar.

Sehar starts to cry. "No, please? Please, no? My baby—"

"I give you one minute. I told you I will ask for something. You have a few seconds. Now decide."

Sehar nods. There's no time for further argument.

"Now, I need everyone to leave the room and close the door behind you," Yamini says calmly.

Epilogue

Amya is giggling and clapping her hands. The little monkey doing tricks on the street is delightful. He jumps up and down and rolls over on command. She wants to feed him bananas that she has inside the house. His keeper smiles and encourages the child to do so, but to be careful.

"He is very unpredictable. He is happy one minute and sad the next."

Amya begins to hum. "Pal pal dil ke pas, tum rehti ho." Every moment you are close to my heart.

"Where did you learn that song, child? That song is older than your grandfather," the monkey's keeper asks.

"Oh, I don't know. I hear it in my heart. But Mama says not to tell people that. It sounds weird." Amya laughs and gets busy feeding the monkey.

"Amya, come on in, child. It's time to eat."

Amya hears her mother's voice, and quickly waves goodbye to the monkey and his keeper. She hands him the few rupees. "Come tomorrow, I will give you extra money."

Inside, Amya stops for a moment and looks at the framed picture of Yamini on the prayer altar. The picture is garlanded, and every morning and night, Sehar lights a diya.

"It is my way of saying thanks and offering prayers to her. She gave up her life for you and your father. She is like a Goddess to me," Sehar tells Amya, it seems on a daily basis.

Amya smiles at the picture. To her, Yamini looked like a movie star. She should have been an actress or a model on the cover of one of the fancy magazines that her mother reads.

"Wash your hands, Amya. God alone knows what diseases that monkey carries," Sehar says as she lays out Amya's favorite meal. Noodles tossed with butter and topped with baby tomatoes and a side of toast with, yes, more butter.

Amya skips merrily to the bathroom. She's so proud of herself. She can now reach the sink without the silly footstool. She washes her hands carefully and dries them on her favorite pink towel.

"Oh, I love these noodles, Mama," she says as she sits on the table and sees the delightful meal.

Rishi emerges from the bedroom and kisses the top of Amya's head. "My baby, you deserve the best."

"Come eat with me, Papa."

"I will for sure. But for breakfast tomorrow. I have to go out now. I will be back late tonight. I am teaching a late class. I love you, baby. You be good and listen to your mom." He kisses her again and then turns and kisses Sehar on the lips. "I love you, honey."

"I love you too. Is it a full class tonight?" Sehar hugs him tight.

"Yes, yes it is. All the students are coming in despite the bad rains."

Sehar hears the new baby crying. She goes to the room and picks up the little one.

"Radha, you are my sweet girl. Why are you crying? Come, come. I got you." The room is filled with the scent of frangipani.

Sehar brings the baby to the main room.

Rishi smiles. He kisses all three of them, waves, and leaves to fulfill his duties.

A small golden candle peeks out of the backpack Rishi has slung over one arm.

Glossary

Amrit (name) – immortality

astha – hope or belief

baba (honorific) – wise old man

baoli – a large, deep well with steps leading down and into the
water

bauji (form of address) – father

beej mantra – the seed sound that works miracles

beeji (form of address) –mother or grandmother

Begur (place name) – village near Bangalore, site of an ancient
fort and temples with sculptures and crumbling
monuments to heroes from its history

Bhagvad Gita – "the Song of God"; Hindu scripture

bhang – an edible preparation of cannabis

bindi – the colored dot worn in the middle of the forehead at
the location of the sixth chakra (area of concentrated
energy)

Bollywood – the Hindi cinema industry, known worldwide as a source of epic costume musicals and melodramas

Bombaim (place name) – "good little bay" in Portuguese, possible source of "Bombay" (Mumbai)

Bon Bibi (name) – guardian spirit of the forest

Chand (name) – the Moon God

Chattarpur (place name) – a well-off section south of Delhi with many beautiful properties (farms)

chawl – low-quality tenement housing for the poor

chuwarak – a strong homemade alcohol, distilled from pineapple

dadi– grandmother

Damini (name) – lightning

Dharavi (place name) – a neighborhood in Mumbai, considered to be one of the largest, most densely populated slums in Asia

Divya (name) – divine brilliance

diya – small cup-shaped oil lamp made of clay

Dokhin Rai [also Dakshin Rai] (name) – a God who rules over beasts and demons

Dronanagri (place name) – "abode of Drona" (a great teacher from the Mahabharata epic era), an ancient city in in the

Himalayas, considered one of the most perfect places to live; also called Dehradun

daayan – witch

gandhak jal –water (jal) that smells of sulphur (gandhak)

Ganesh (name) –the elephant-headed God

ganja – marijuana; cannabis

Gayatri mantra – a universal prayer expressing hope for enlightenment

gulmohar tree – a tree with an umbrella-like canopy and stunning scarlet flowers; also called royal poinciana

Hejaz and Najd (place names) – currently, parts of the Kingdom of Saudi Arabia; the holy city of Mecca is located in Hejaz

hisalu – the tiny Himalayan golden raspberry

jaggery – a coarse dark brown sugar made by evaporation of the sap of palm trees

Jako rahke Saiyan, mar sake Na Koi – "He is my savior and I believe He will protect me"

Jigyasa (name) – one who is curious to know

Kali Gad – river named for the Goddess Kali

kaphal – bayberry bush; its berry is consumed like a sour dried raspberry

karma – the sum of a person's actions in this and previous states of existence, viewed as deciding their fate in future existences

Lakshmi (name) – Goddess of prosperity, good luck, and beauty

Madhuja (name) – made of honey

mala – a string of 108 beads used in meditation

mantra – a mystical formula of invocation or incantation

Meera (name) – sea or ocean; a 16th-century Hindu princess who selflessly dedicated her life to Lord Krishna

Nakuru (place name) – city in the Great Rift Valley of Kenya; location of Lake Nakuru National Park, home to African wildlife and thousands of flamingos

namaste – a respectful greeting; literally, "I bow to you"

Nirvana – in Buddhism, the state of bliss that transcends suffering, karma, and samsara (the indefinitely repeated cycles of birth, misery, and death) through the extinction of desire and individual consciousness

Padang Bai (place name) – seaside town in Bali, known for pure white sand beaches and Blue Lagoon

pakora – a piece of meat or vegetable dipped in batter and fried; fritter

Pal pal dil ke pas, tum rehti ho – "Every moment you are close to my heart"

poori aloo – deep-fried unleavened bread made of whole wheat flour (poori) stuffed with potato (aloo)

Prasad (name) – gracious gift

prasadam – sacred food first offered to God, and then to worshippers

Radha (name) – Goddess of love, compassion, and devotion; the epitome of eternal love

Rohit Bal (name) – award-winning, internationally known contemporary fashion designer based in New Delhi

roti – a round flatbread cooked on a griddle; may be used as a wrapper for other food

Rumi (name) – 13th-century Sufi mystic and poet, writing in Persian and Arabic, still revered for his lyrical poems

sadhu – a holy man, sage, or ascetic

Sahastradhara (place name) – "thousand-fold spring," a collection of natural pools where water drips from limestone stalactites, turning it into medicinal sulphur springs

saree – a garment of an elaborately draped length of cotton or silk

Sea Link Bridge – bridge linking parts of Mumbai along the Arabian Sea, opened in 2009, with striking modern architecture

Shahajahanabad (place name) – city founded in 1639 by Shah Jahan as the new Mughal capital after Agra; current-day Old Delhi

Shakti (name) – sacred force or empowerment; primordial cosmic energy; the personification of divine female power

sirki grass – wicker, reed, or cane, with hollow slender stalks

softy – soft-serve ice cream

Soma (name) – the elixir goddess known to relieve pain

sparsh – touch

stupa – a mound- or dome-like structure containing Buddhist relics, used as a place of meditation

subhisaj – heal well

svikroti – acceptance; approval

Tagore (name) – Rabindranath Tagore, a Bengali poet, writer, and composer of the late 19th and early 20th centuries, influential for introducing Indian culture to the West and vice versa

Tapkeshwar Temple – located in a cave near Dronanagri; named for the water that drips from a nearby rock, with

the ability to grant the wishes of those who seek Lord
Shiva's blessing

The Pink City – Jaipur, India, so called for the uniformly terra
cotta pink buildings; pink is the considered the color of
purity and kindness

Vedic – relating to the Vedas, early religious texts that inform
Hinduism; scripture or holy writ concerning the nature of
the Divine

virohana – to heal

wedding samagri list – those items needed to perform marriage
rituals

Yamini (name) – starry night; light in the darkness

yogi – a Hindu ascetic seeking self-liberation through bodily
and mental disciplines, sometimes credited with
supernormal powers

Also by Monica Bhide

Inspirational Books

In Conversation with Exceptional Women (ebook)

Read, Write, Reflect (Bodes Well Publishing, 2018)

Fiction and Short Stories

Karma and the Art of Butter Chicken (Bodes Well Publishing, 2016)

The Devil In Us (2014)

The Soul Catcher (Bodes Well Publishing, 2017)

Tattletales (Bodes Well Publishing 2017)

Food Essays and Cookbooks

A Life of Spice (2015)

Modern Spice: Inspired Indian Flavors for the Contemporary Kitchen (Simon and Schuster. 2009; Random House India, 2010)

The Everything Indian Cookbook: 300 Tantalizing Recipes from Sizzling Tandoor Chicken to Fiery Lamb Vindaloo (Adams Media, 2004)

Monica's essays have been included in *Best Food Writing 2005, 2009, 2010,* and *2014,* edited by Holly Hughes (Da Capo Press)

Monica's books are available through Amazon.com, BN.com, Kobo, iBooks and her website, MonicaBhide.com

Made in the USA
Middletown, DE
03 September 2021